*Totally Bound Publishing books by Raven McAllan and Cassie O'Brien*

**The Scots and the Sassenachs**
The Earl of Callander's Secret Bride

*Totally Bound Publishing books by Raven McAllan*

**Single Books**
Hong Kong Heat
Taken Identity
Fairground Attraction
The Duke's Temptation
The Viscount Meets his Match

**Diomhair**
Secrets Shared
Secrets Uncovered
Secrets Remembered
Secrets Dispatched
Secrets Learned
Secrets Dispelled

**Daring Ladies**
The Earl and The Courtesan

**Castle on the Loch**
Love by the Stroke of Midnight

**Anthologies**
Bully for You: Chasing Charlie

**Collections**
A Little Bit Cupid: For One Night Only

*Totally Bound Publishing books by Cassie O'Brien*

**Single Books**
The Girls' Club
From a Lady to a Maid
Ellie's Rules

The Scots and the Sassenachs

# THE EARL OF CALLANDER'S SECRET BRIDE

RAVEN MCALLAN &
CASSIE O'BRIEN

The Earl of Callander's Secret Bride
ISBN # 978-1-83943-749-6

Interior text design by Claire Siemaszkiewicz
Totally Bound Publishing



Published in 2021 by Totally Bound Publishing, United Kingdom.



Totally Bound Publishing is an imprint of Totally Entwined Group Limited.

# THE EARL OF CALLANDER'S SECRET BRIDE

# Dedication

To Leslie O'Brien for her words of encouragement
and nagging, and
Wendy Martin who is the best cheerleader ever.
Thank you both for your support.

# Chapter One

Lady Cairstine McColl knew it was wrong to slip out from her family home unnoticed and go for a long tramp across the hills. Nevertheless, after the news her papa had just imparted, she'd had to get away. It was that or completely lose her temper. Shout, scream and be the termagant she didn't want to be. She acknowledged it had been a close-run thing. Hence her escape. A pity she couldn't escape the future as easily.

*How could he?*

She skirted the three large boulders that edged the head of the loch and jumped over the burn that flowed into it with a gurgle as it danced across the stony bottom. In winter, when it was in full spate, she would have had no chance. Now in June, when the nights were short and daylight hours long, the weather was sometimes drier and the burn no more than a trickle.

Cairstine strode up the slopes to where the forest began, her boots giving her purchase on the slippery rocks. It might not have rained recently, but these slopes were always damp and covered in moss. As she walked, she mulled over her papa's words.

*How,* how *could he?*

He had promised her in marriage to an Englishman. An *Englishman!* Whom she had never met. *How draconian.* And how undoubtedly, in this so-called enlightened age, unacceptable. Surely she should at least have met the man and decided if this marriage of convenience was for her?

Sadly, her papa had been unmoved by her pleas. He'd simply told her she would leave for England in five days' time.

*England. Who on earth would want to go there? And to a place called* Corbridge*? Not even London, or Carlisle.* Until she'd studied a book of maps in the library she'd had no idea where Corbridge was. Evidently between Newcastle and Carlisle. A market town, near the site of the wall built in Roman times to keep the Scots out of England. What a pity it was no longer used for the same purpose. That would have meant there was no way she could have been forced to head south.

According to a pamphlet she'd found on the desk—it seemed her papa had been investigating—this Corbridge was a pretty well set-up place with lots of new and imposing buildings sitting side by side with older, equally as imposing ones.

She couldn't have cared less. It wouldn't matter what it was like, it was not *home.*

George Armstrong, she thought in disgust. An *Armstrong.* One of those murdering, thieving Border Reivers of old who had thought nothing of riding from England into Scotland to steal the cattle of good honest Scotsmen—and women. The family names of the marauding bands were still notorious enough to put the fear of God into anyone who lived within a day's ride of the border even in these modern times. Cairstine had been raised on stories of Scots venturing as far as Yorkshire, and the English to Edinburgh. All in retaliation for some real or imagined wrongdoing. You had to be thankful such days were over—but that made her papa's demands even harder to fathom.

Worse though than the raids—if it was possible for anything *to* be worse—Armstrong was a Sassenach with, he was said to boast, not one jot of Scottish blood in him. Where was the common ground?

Why, oh why had her papa thought she'd be happy married to one of *them*?

If he had thought at all. These last couple of weeks he'd been preoccupied, less likely to chat or ask what she had been doing, and never sharing his day with her. Not at all the man she had adored for so many years.

*How could he? Is he demented?* When the name of her prospective husband was enough to put fear into even the bravest of people... She was no different.

She shuddered and gathered her breath for the final steep few yards to her favourite place on the estate. The lookout. Where in times gone by a sentry would have been placed to keep guard for enemies.

Now she was the only one who ever went there.

Or so she'd imagined.

Head down, deep in thought, she ploughed into a tree.

A very human tree, which swayed before it steadied again.

She scowled. Of all the people it could be it had to be Duncan Callander. Her neighbour, her...her what? She had no idea except that he was the one man who made her skin tighten in an arousing way and made her wonder...what if?

A child of the countryside, she was no stranger to the way animals mated and had on more than one occasion caught sight of a man and a woman in the undergrowth, the lady's skirts kilted around her waist, his trews around his ankles. It wasn't something she'd contemplated doing herself though—until recently.

"Where's where the enemy? Who do I have to shoot?" Duncan grabbed her arm with one hand to rescue her from falling on her rump, put his other hand to his forehead and scanned the area with an extravagant movement. "Pistol or bow and arrow?"

Cairstine giggled. Trust Duncan to cheer her up. "The culprit is too far to reach with either," she said glumly as she smoothed her skirts down and remembered what had sent her to the lookout in a rush. "In England, at a place called Corbridge."

"Corbridge?" he said as he dropped his hand from his face. The confusion in his eyes mirrored the incredulous tone of his voice. "Why in hades Corbridge? What the hell's going on?"

Cairstine sighed. "Hell just about sums it up. My papa says I am to marry the black-hearted devil that is George Armstrong."

Duncan's jaw clenched as she said the name. *George Armstrong of Corbridge…the bastard!* Not that he had ever met the man, but the fame—or infamy—of the Armstrong family was well known and noted in the annals of history. Around a hundred years earlier they had been given a baronetcy—under somewhat suspicious circumstances—and they revelled in their reputation.

Blood raced through his veins at the thought of Cairstine in the clutches of such a man. She stood close enough to kiss, her lips mere inches from his own.

Another part of his anatomy stirred deep within his trews with an emotion other than anger. The heady scent of her teased his nostrils and he sniffed the air. Violets, he decided—sweet and seductively entrancing like the lady herself.

He dropped his hands to his sides against an urge to sweep her into his arms and assure her he would not allow the marriage to take place. He was powerless to prevent it—Cairstine's father's title being higher ranked in the natural order than his own. What was he, as an earl compared to a duke? Instead he concentrated on not curling his hands into fists and asked with a calmness he didn't feel, "When and where is this event to take place?"

Cairstine gazed at him, a question written in her eyes as if she sensed the power of the emotions running through his body. "I leave for Corbridge in five days. Oh, Duncan, something is wrong, and I have no idea what it could be. I have asked Papa to explain his decision, but all he says it I have to do this thing. Why?" She whirled around and her skirts followed her, giving him a tantalizing glimpse of a well-turned ankle visible above her half boot. How he wished it showed more.

*Callander, get your mind out of the gutters.*

"What on earth could be going on?" Cairstine asked in a plaintive tone that hit him hard. "Duncan, I'm at my wit's end. I cannot move him."

Duncan nodded, his mind busy with possible plans, and he turned to one side, needing time to think of ways and means to execute them as well as considering the likely consequences. "Stay strong. I'm off to check my snares and have a think. Don't worry, I will see you again before you go. Can you be here at the same time tomorrow?"

Cairstine nodded. "I will make sure I am."

Duncan nodded. "Until then." He spun on his heels and set off in the direction of his manor a mile or so distant on the opposite hill, his thoughts in a whirl.

*What in hades is her father up to*? To date, the Duke of Glenard, known as Lord Nathaniel McColl in these parts, had been a loving and somewhat protective father to his only daughter.

He strode on. The smell of pine resin carried on the warmth of the June breeze replaced the scent of violets in his nose, but Duncan hardly noticed as he began to gather his thoughts. A rescue plan was needed, one that would absolve Cairstine from all blame so as not to leave her in her parent's bad graces. Or give any hint of collusion between the two of them. She should not guess his part in it, to allow her to answer with perfect honesty if questioned later by her father.

A bold idea occurred and he quickened his pace while contemplating the prospects and pitfalls of it. A disguise would be required so she didn't immediately recognise him. It would ruin everything if she inadvertently gave his identity away to anyone with her. Plus, he needed to decide on a place of safety for her to pass the time until his plan achieved its aim.

Cairstine stared after Duncan with a sinking feeling settling in the pit of her stomach. She had been so sure he was going to speak out in her defence, offer to reason with her father, add his voice to hers.

And he hadn't. *Why not?*

He was Duncan. Her playmate when they were young. Yes, he had annoyed her, teased her and generally treated her as if she were there for his entertainment, but she had known, was *certain,* he was her champion. There for her.

Perhaps not like the time he tied her Celtic-red pigtails around a tree branch and left her. That had made her hopping mad. He'd come back of course, by which time she'd lost a clump of hair trying to get free. But as well as teasing her in many ways, he'd championed her. Taught her to guddle fish, to set snares and to scrump for apples. How to apply dock leaves when she'd fallen into a clump of stinging nettles when they were running out of the field where the best mushrooms grew along the hedgerow and Farmer McCullum's bull lived.

Duncan had held her head when she was sick from eating too many wild blackberries, and sneaked her into the house, unseen, when she'd fallen in the burn and was dripping wet. That had earned her a scolding from her nurse, but not from her parents, who would certainly have forbidden her to do all the things she had enjoyed if they had known.

He'd encouraged her to ride astride without a saddle, taught her how to grip the horse and sail over fences and hedges. Never judgmental and always supportive. So why had he not commented more this time? Surely this was a bigger, more important thing to get involved with?

Cairstine sighed and sat for a few more minutes as she gazed, abstracted, without really seeing anything, in the direction he'd gone. Why was life so unfair? Up until the day before she'd had very clear ideas on what she hoped to do, and that had included staying with her Aunt Senga in Edinburgh at the elegant Georgian town house she and her husband owned in the New Town. She had so looked forwards to attending assemblies in the company of her cousin Jean—a year older—along with various suppers and musicales, and maybe the following year—a Season in London. Not that London particularly appealed, but she would like to see how a come out there differed from one in the Scottish capital. It would all be information to carry into her future. And maybe her prospective husband would have followed her to Town to court her just as he should, before approaching her papa to ask for her hand. *Not like Armstrong.*

Now all those hopes and dreams were dashed.

With a sigh that went all the way down to her boots, she stood up, brushed down her gown and began to retrace her steps. Perhaps she should try to reason with her parent again?

If only her mama were alive, things might have been different. Papa had never before been an unreasonable man, and her mama had always been able to negotiate with him. Now things were not so simple. However, Cairstine reasoned with herself, she had to try.

Mind made up, she increased her pace and headed for home.

Her luck was in. As she crossed the wide stone hallway, her boots clacking on the flags, her papa came out of his study.

He saw her, started and began to retrace his steps.

"Papa." Cairstine's sharp tone stopped him in his tracks. It was now or never. "We have to talk. Now," she added before he began to protest. "Or I swear I will not be here when you want me to go south."

He shut his mouth with a snap and frowned. Cairstine forced herself to continue.

"I deserve some reasons why you wish me to do such a terrible thing. And do not trot out that old, old non-reason of 'as your daughter, I should do as you say'. We live in more enlightened times now." She wasn't sure they did, but had no intention of adding—'or we should do'. She was determined to appear and sound adult and reasonable. "Please, Papa, I know there is more to this than meets the eye. If you want my help, I need to know why." She took the few steps needed to reach him. "Or I will be the most intractable child ever to have lived."

Her papa sighed. "Yes, you need to know, and as for intractability? I do not doubt that for one minute. Come into the study. We won't be disturbed there." The expression on his face sent a frisson of fear skittering though her. Something terrible had happened.

Cairstine waited until they were sat each side of the fire. Even in June, the study with its thick walls, built to withstand the cold Scottish winters, needed a fire to keep away the dampness. The day was what local folk called dreich. Cloudy, damp and a with hint of drizzle. A day when the warmth of the glowing coals was welcome.

"Well, Papa?" she said gently. "Surely the words 'a secret shared is a burden halved' are true?"

"Sometimes, not always." His face was stern. "I wish it was."

Not for the first time, she wondered what was going on in her papa's head of late. "Well, we won't know until you say what's bothering you. So now is the time. I meant what I said. I refuse to go anywhere without knowing why."

Lord McColl straightened in his chair. "This paints my father in a bad light. A very bad light. But he was young and foolish, a hot-headed Jacobite who forgot the first tenet of rebellion. *Never write anything down*."

Her heart sank. It appeared worse than she thought. "Treason?"

"Not quite. You know of course about the Bear Gates of Traquair House?" he asked, then shook his head. "Of course you do."

Cairstine nodded. The story was engrained into every Scot's heart, be they a supporter or not. It had been drummed into her when she was still in the nursery. How once Bonnie Prince Charlie rode away from his cousin the gates were closed, never to be opened until a Stuart king was once more on the throne.

"My father wrote a letter to the Laird of Traquair, to pledge his support to Charles Edward Stuart. Somehow it has got into the hands of Armstrong. Now the bugger says unless you marry him, he will say it was written by me—and he could get away with doing so. It is signed by way of our title, without a Christian name to distinguish the difference between father and son. For it to be penned by my father might be forgiven. After all it was many years ago and a not-inconsiderable number of Scotsmen were sympathizers. However, if it is purported to come from me, the outcome would be very bad indeed. You would be utterly ruined, and that I could not bear." He took a deep breath, pain evident in his eyes. "For myself? I do not know, but at worse I could be arrested and our estate confiscated by the Crown. Then who would take you to wife, with your reputation in tatters and you penniless to boot? No. I have tormented myself. I had hoped to be approached with a very different offer for you, but he has not done so, and I'm out of time. There is no way round it. Better a husband, even if it is George Armstrong, than risk leaving you destitute."

"Oh, Papa." Cairstine bit back a sob—for herself or him she had no idea—and leapt up to put her arms around him. "I cannot bear to see you in this fix. I will do as you say and go." *And hunt out that letter and destroy it.* What else she would do she would decide as and when a decision was needed. The one thing she did not intend to do was marry Armstrong. "It will all work out, Papa. I promise."

He nodded and patted her arm. "If only there were another way, but there isn't, I'm afraid, my dear."

What next? She dared not share her knowledge with anyone except Duncan, and to be honest she had no idea how he could help her. But if anyone could, it would be him. "It will all work out," she said again. Whether to reassure herself or her papa she had no idea.

# Chapter Two

Duncan's pace quickened as soon as the grey stone walls of his country home came into view. Far less grand than his ancestral pile, his hunting lodge had only twenty rooms, and was all the more comfortable for being so.

He entered the great hall and hollered his general factotum's name, not bothering to mind his language inside a house where no ladies resided. "Bruce… I have a bugger of a thirst on me. Bring a quart of ale, please."

His chief steward limped into the hall more than fifteen minutes later carrying the two-pint pot in his one good hand while Duncan sat debating in his high-backed chair whether he should just go in search of his own drink. He looked at Bruce as he set the tankard down on the table within his master's reach. "Your leg is loupin today?" He should have thought about that. It was damp. Driech, as they said thereabouts. Of course it would pain him.

Taciturn and dour, his servant answered with a grunt and nod. "Ay, it's a wee bittie sair, but naething tae fash yersel oer." As ever, when Bruce was in pain his accent became stronger. At times so much so that Duncan had trouble understanding him.

Duncan frowned. "Then you should have sent Robbie in with my ale and rested. Hell, man, I want you fit and well, not out of action."

"I'm nae fit fer the rubbish heap as yet, yer ken. Anyhoo, he's away with the beasts to the top field. Lachy's turned his ankle."

*Fine master I am. The man's in pain and I'm sending him all over the house when I have two good limbs and could easily go myself.*

Duncan nodded. The estate ran with far fewer workers than many, and most could turn their hand to anything. Lachy, the farm manager, had slipped from a ladder the previous week, ignored the pain in his ankle until he could no longer put any weight on it and now paid the price.

He knew he should retire Bruce and give the position to his younger and fitter son, Robbie, but he could not bring himself to dismiss the man or ease him into retirement. Bruce had followed Duncan's elder brother Fraser into the 93rd Sutherland Highland regiment as his batman, then into France before finally bringing Fraser's body home after the battle of *Quatre Bras,* even though grievously injured himself. On more than one occasion he had insisted his job was to serve his master and that he would do so until his dying breath—even if both Robbie and Duncan did their best to shield him from the most arduous duties.

Still, Duncan mused, if marriage was on his, Duncan's, mind, his prospective bride might insist on one of those new-fangled butler types rather than a general steward. It was true Bruce suited an all-male household not over-bothered with the niceties that meant so much to the ladies, but he would never be forced out.

Duncan knew his mama would have had Bruce installed in an estate-owned cottage with a pension long before now, but the arrival of Fraser's corpse back at his ancestral home had finished off their father by way of a massive apoplexy and his broken-hearted widow had followed her husband to the graveyard not six months later. A cruel twist of fate that in some ways had been for the best. His mother would never have been able to cope without his father's guidance, and he could never have hoped to compete with his papa's memory. Harsh though it was, this way his mama was happy—or at least not around to upset him, the staff and their neighbours with her pious and self-pitying attitude. It was hard to imagine how those two things were able to coexist, but in his mother, they'd managed.

At least now he could pick up the pieces and carry on.

Duncan dismissed his steward with a wave of his hand and a word of thanks and lifted his tankard. He drank deeply then wiped the foam from his top lip with the sleeve of his shirt and returned his thoughts to the matter currently exercising his mind.

*Cairstine.*

Cairstine had never been seen as a prospective bride for him. She was far too high-born to be given in marriage to a younger son. He remembered her red hair plaited into pigtails, the smattering of freckles across her nose which she'd in no way found attractive but he'd always thought were quite pretty. She'd tagged along behind him whenever she could. Smaller and several years younger but determined not to be left behind, she'd joined him in any adventure he'd cared to lead her on. Then she had grown womanly curves, the sight of which caused his heart to pump harder and his blood to race through his veins.

He jumped to his feet, impatient now to put in hand the practical elements of his plan that could be accomplished in advance and strode from the room. It was too late to do anything much that day. Stirling, the nearest town, was a good twenty-miles ride, and he had his doubts that he could find what he needed there. It would have to be Glasgow, thirty-odd miles south.

* * * *

After a troubled night's sleep, he was up at the crack of dawn.

He headed for the kitchen, where it was too early for even the cook to be around, filched a slab of cheese and a hunk of bread and left the house just as the sun rose over the Ben—the mountain behind his house.

Once in the stables, he saddled his mount and rode out for Glasgow in solitary state, not caring to take a groom along to bear witness to his business there. Some things were best done alone.

His search for a supplier of ecclesiastical wear was fruitless—were they all heathens in the area?—but he found what he sought in a shop that provided costumes to those of the Glaswegian aristocracy who might attend a ball being held in the style of a fancy-dress Masquerade. There he purchased two sets of monk's robes and added a couple of masks, which would hide most of their faces. Those garments, along with other essentials, would stow easily in two saddlebags. He satisfied the shopkeeper's curiosity by saying he hoped to go to a bacchanalia up in the north, later in the year.

While he gathered items to pack, Duncan racked his brains for a way to soothe Cairstine's fears when he met her the following day. He could imagine her reaction if he admitted he'd thought of a solution to sabotage the marriage plans but would not relay the details of it because she was better off not knowing them for her own good.

Would it be best to stay silent and pretend he was still trying to discover a solution?

The hours of darkness brought him no closer to what he should divulge other than to offer his reassurance he would find a way to help and ask her to place her trust in him.

At daybreak, Duncan broke his fast with a mug of ale and a mutton pastry and left the manor. He headed up the hill to where the sun was just rising over the horizon and turning every dewdrop into a sparkling crystal, every cobweb into a lacy delight. For once he hardly noticed those things he usually revelled in.

He crested the hill and realised Cairstine had arrived at the lookout before him.

As soon as he saw her he noticed a change in her demeanour from the day before. A fresh breeze blew through the curls of her red hair, but that was the only thing ruffled about her. She turned to face him, her gaze steady and calm, with a defiant tilt to her chin that gave her an air of quiet determination.

"You have always stood by my side, Duncan, and I thank you for it. But I have persuaded Papa to speak his mind and now know his reasoning," she said before he could even utter a greeting. "The resolution to my dilemma is within my own grasp and there is nothing you could do in my place that could not be better done by myself." Her voice was quiet, but her tone and her stance so determined he wanted to hug her.

In that moment he knew he loved her and no other wife would do. Defiant and brave as a lion, she captured his heart and soul, although Duncan acknowledged it was not the moment to declare himself. She needed his help, whether she knew it or not, and he took his dismissal with a small smile. "Then my every good wish for success in your endeavours. I will await news of the outcome." What else could he say? That he intended to discover for himself why she'd decided his help was no longer needed? What it was all about? And whatever she thought, he intended to be her champion.

Duncan took Cairstine's hand and kissed it gently before he turned away in the direction of his manor, silently kicking himself for not proposing to her when he inherited the title. But she had been so excited at the thought of a few months in Edinburgh he had held back, while making plans to follow her there. He had intended to rent a house and woo her with the added bonus of being on hand to sabotage the plans of any other rival seeking to engage her affections. Now he had to think differently. *Time to step up to the mark.* His plans grew and solidified as he thought of Cairstine being at the mercy of the devious bastard, Armstrong. Whatever the reason—and somehow he needed to discover what that was—it could not be good enough.

He arrived home and called the name of Bruce's son, loud and clear. The younger steward, Robbie Logan, took less than three minutes to enter the hall. "Aye, m'lord?"

"I have a task for you. In four days, you'll accompany me on a secret raid. Tell no one about it, including your father. Say we're off to look over some cattle or some such thing." He knew he could rely on Robbie to do as he was asked, and with credibility. Many times over the years they had plotted and enjoyed adventures together, usually—though not always—with a favourable result. He prayed this was one of their successful ploys. "Use your imagination." He laughed. "It's one of your most effective assets."

Robbie bowed. "Aye, m'lord." He grinned. "Nothing awfy, eh?"

"As you say. In the morning, ride to the bothy on the farthest edge of the Leithen estate and ensure it is fit for human habitation." He remembered how even on the warmest of nights the bothy, on the edge of one of his lesser properties, remained cool. "I accept it will be two days' hard riding there and back but needs must. Stock it with food, drink, firewood and blankets, enough of each to last several days. I know time is tight, but it is of the essence."

Robbie nodded. "Ye may rely on ma discretion."

Duncan permitted himself a small smile. "Of that, I am sure. Report your progress to me tomorrow evening. And my thanks."

Robbie turned. Duncan watched him leave the room and drained the last of his ale. "Now…" he muttered under his breath. "We keep watch and wait for her to depart."

* * * *

Cairstine settled in her seat and let her feet curl around the hot brick under them. It was ridiculous to need one in June, but the day was wet and chilly and she appreciated it.

The weather mimicked her mood.

Unsettled. Unpleasant. Unsure. She sighed as her papa glanced at her. They were the only the two occupants inside the vehicle as her lady's maid had refused point-blank to accompany her and had declared, *"I'll nae set foot on Sassenach land. Dinae ask it"*.

Perhaps it was for the best. The fewer people around, the less likelihood of her plans going awry.

"I sometimes wonder where your grandfather's brain was at when he set such controversial thoughts down on paper," he said as the carriage left the glen and headed towards Stirling. "He wasn't in general a stupid man, so why on earth write a damned letter that even at the time could have landed him in deep hot water?"

Cairstine hugged him. "Did you know it even existed before Armstrong used it as leverage?"

He shook his head. "No, and I would rather have suspected it to be a work of fiction, a forgery, if I hadn't been sent a copy of the content along with a small snippet cut from the page of the original to prove it was his handwriting."

"No room for doubt then." She sighed. "Will you tell me all you know about George Armstrong and his forebears? Forewarned is forearmed." *There were a lot of fores in that mouthful, Let's hope that's a positive sign.*

"The Armstrongs," Nathaniel McColl began. "In days gone by, that name would have struck terror into any Scotsman who lived near the border. Once they lived on our side of the border, but some became heathens and went south. Murdering, cattle rustling, turncoats. Their ancestors were moss troupers, those men who when beaten refused to be banished to Fermanagh and stayed hidden." He swallowed then winced as if the words that followed were painful to admit. "Thence to do as they pleased in defiance of all that was proposed with regards to their exile across the sea. You might not like them, but you have to commend them for their loyalty to their land and people. They became barons and some say there's more than a mystery in how *that* title came to be theirs."

Cairstine could believe that, but not that they could be commended in any way. How could you commend someone who blackmailed someone else for their own ends? However, she held her peace and merely asked, "Why me?"

"In the main, for your dowry and the wealth you will inherit when I die. With your mama only bearing one child, everything not entailed will go to you. He needs money, and by whatever method it fell into his hands, I suspect the letter was a godsend."

That was a lever she might be able to use. "Gambling?"

"Not him, his late brother Alun. An unscrupulous reprobate who tried to bleed the estate dry before he was killed in a duel by someone who suspected him of cheating while playing cards. Whether his death was justified or not, it was the best outcome for the family if truth be told, for he was a bad penny if ever there was one. Rumour has it there is now little money for the upkeep of the estate, and their harvest last year was bad. It looks not to be faring any better this year, leaving the family in dire straits. From memory, their land is not naturally green and even sheep struggle to find enough grazing to sustain them. In years past, before Alun began his ruinous career of cards and dice, they owned many more fertile acres, but Alun sold them to pay his gambling debts without thought for his family or the people who depend on them to make their living."

"Those poor people to have their lives in danger due to the avarice of one man." Cairstine bit her lip. It was not as cut and dried as she had thought. "How do you know all this?"

Nathaniel McColl shrugged. "I made it my business to find out. I even offered money to try and buy him off. To no avail. And now I cannot escape the suspicion there is more to this feud, affair of the letter, call it what you will. That this business is also of a more personal nature that runs a good deal deeper. I just do not know exactly as to how or why, though I do have my suspicions, of course."

Despite the seriousness of the situation, Cairstine was intrigued. She wriggled to settle more comfortably on the squabs, sensing a mystery. Her papa was a good raconteur, so be it sad or happy, she reckoned she was in for an entertaining few minutes. "Deeper how?"

Her papa steepled his hands and looked at her over the top of them with a small smile. "Ah, well, there you have it. Plots, stratagem and unrequited love. I'm going back several generations here, you understand. To my however-many-times-removed grandmother. Who, so family history goes, was visiting her friend in the borders when a local laird, or is it lord down there, I'm never sure, saw her and fell in love. Or so the family lore says."

"And…?" There had to be more. Cairstine leant forwards the better to listen. "What happened?"

"He promptly decided the woman he was supposed to wed was no longer the one for him. That woman was an Armstrong, who I was told went into a decline, was married off to someone else and became a harridan."

It had all the makings of the sort of gothic tale Cairstine enjoyed, except it appeared to be no fiction. "Oh dear. And your however-many-times-removed grandmama. Did she marry him?"

Nathaniel shook his head. "She gave him short shrift, told him she was betrothed anyway and had no intention of reneging. So not only was the Armstrong woman left alone, so was her erstwhile swain. He promptly married a member of the Hetherington family, who were at loggerheads with the Armstrongs, so thus added insult to injury. That is when, according to folklore, their fortunes began to dwindle."

"Oh my goodness." *What a story!* "Bad blood indeed. Do you think this is revenge?"

"The only thing I'm sure of is that this is about more than just money," Nathaniel said gloomily. "I have no real idea of what George Armstrong's true motive is but I would guess some kind of personal payback is involved, wouldn't you?"

Cairstine had to agree. As the coach trundled towards Edinburgh she mulled over her papa's words. Was it enough to cause upsets all these years on? If so, her task could be harder than she'd thought. At least she had plenty of time to think over her various options. Corbridge couldn't be reached in a day.

She was still pondering those options as they approached the outskirts of Linlithgow. It had been a long day and the seat in the carriage became harder as time went on. Her papa had decided to drive all the way to Edinburgh, the Scottish capital, in the shortest possible time. Even after a brief stop for lunch and to stretch their legs, Cairstine was weary and stiff as they approached the inn her papa had chosen for them to stay at overnight.

They arrived just as the shadows lengthened and the lamps around the door were lit.

For one brief second a shape flitted across the entrance to the stable yard. Cairstine stared. Was the outline familiar or was it wishful thinking?

# Chapter Three

Duncan received word from the lad he had sent to watch the road that the McColl carriage was on the move. He called for Robbie to saddle up their mounts, knowing they had time to catch up with a slow, lumbering coach with only one road able to bear its load for its occupants to travel south in any degree of comfort.

They came up behind it and stayed far enough to its rear not to attract the notice of the coachman or his assistant, should they have had any reason to turn and look behind. A tedious journey ensued as they followed a vehicle that could travel no faster than a horse's gait of slow trot, and Duncan puffed a sigh of relief when the coachman used his whip to point his team towards a coaching inn on the road to Linlithgow. It gave him a moment's satisfaction to discover his idea of where the McColls would put up overnight had been correct. It was the best of the inns on offer, and he'd thought Nathaniel McColl would not scrimp on accommodation, but he hadn't been totally certain.

Duncan signalled to Robbie to cut across country, circle wide of the coach and thus reach the inn ahead of it. They dismounted and led their horses into the stable just as Duncan heard the rumble of wooden wheels on the cobbles of the yard. He paused and glanced over his shoulder, only to find the coach closer than he had expected. Cairstine gazed out of its window, looking in his direction, so he ducked out of sight behind the timbered half-door. *Hades…that was close!*

He sent Robbie to the innkeeper to reserve his accommodation while he stayed out of sight, and once indoors kept to his room overnight. Robbie, by his own preference, decided not to consign the care of their horses to an unknown ostler and chose accommodation above the stable. Therefore he was able to bring word of the McColl carriage horses being backed into their traces as Duncan, dressed but without his boots on, drank his breakfast ale.

"Then we will be away as soon after they leave as is sensible." Duncan drained his glass, finished his black pudding and made haste to get ready.

They saddled up and followed the coach until Duncan saw a clear stretch of road ahead. Lined with green foliage thick enough to provide cover for them to move ahead of the other vehicle unseen by its occupants, it was the perfect place to set up an ambush. He swerved off the road at a fast gallop, unheeding of rabbit holes or other obstacles, dismounted and handed Robbie a mask, robe and pistol.

"Tether the horses out of view, if you would, then disguise yourself. If I lay across the road as if mortally ill you can kneel beside me as if praying for heavenly intervention."

Robbie grinned. "Would you get it?"

"Probably not, but luckily it doesn't matter. When the coach halts, I will miraculously recover and we can draw our weapons." It had been the best idea he could come up with that he thought might have a chance of succeeding.

"Ah hae you back."

Duncan clapped his friend on the shoulder and took his position, with Robbie on his knees beside him, and waited. A few minutes later the coachman pulled on his reins and halted the vehicle.

"My lord, two men of God lie in our path. Not of our persuasion, but still…?" His voice was clear. Duncan might not be a man of the cloth, or particularly religious, but he thought if ever there were a time to pray, that moment was it.

Nathaniel McColl answered him. "Then step down, man, and aid them."

Duncan watched out of half-closed eyes. The coachman dismounted and, as he'd hoped when he'd made his plan, did not retrieve his weapon from under his box seat, faced only by two monks. He waited for the man to walk closer, then stood and pointed his pistol. Robbie straightened and aimed his own weapon at the footman standing on the back board. The servant held up his hands to offer his surrender and did not reach for the stout cudgel that dangled at his side, attached to his belt by way of a leather thong.

*Thank the Lord.* The fact that the footman would be suitably armed hadn't passed him by, and he had thought disarming him would have to be undertaken swiftly, but the fact the man had done nothing about it had been an added bonus. He nodded to Robbie, who understood it would be up to him to retrieve the cudgel as soon as possible.

Duncan lowered the timbre of his voice to sound unlike his normal softer tone. "Stand and deliver." The gruffness even surprised him.

The coachman jumped and shouted, "Beware, Your Grace! They are not priests. It's an ambush."

"Then do as you are bidden. No heroics are needed." The duke didn't sound as if that pronouncement was what he would have preferred to say. It was, though, something Duncan was happy to hear.

Duncan beckoned the footman to dismount and join his colleague, then handed Robbie his pistol so he had a shot for each should either be brave or foolish enough to try to rush him while his back was turned. He took a deep breath, opened the carriage door, and let it escape when he saw no sign of Cairstine's small, but lethal, silver muff pistol. He grasped her hand and tugged. She stumbled from the coach, regained her footing and gave him an icy stare.

"Unhand me this instant, you black-hearted cur. I wear no jewels of value." If an icy tone could have stopped him, that one would have.

"Sorry." Duncan pulled her towards him. She stiffened, raised her knee, and he hurriedly swerved his hip to avoid her attempt to rearrange his manhood. She struggled in earnest then, seeking to break free of his hold until in desperation Duncan wrapped his arms around her in a bear hug and muttered into her ear, "Stop. It is not my intention to hurt you."

"Remove your hands from me, you filthy dog!" Cairstine spat the words in a sharp staccato manner, her face a study of fury that matched the fiery colour of her hair, leaving Duncan in no doubt that if she held a dagger it would now be between his ribs. "You are *not* sorry."

She tilted her head to peer beneath his monk's cowl, and although his face was covered by a mask, something she saw seemed to give her pause. She narrowed her eyes and tapped her foot. "Hmm..."

Duncan waited for her renewed resistance, but it did not come, although her stance remained wary, on the edge of flight. He took advantage of what after all might only be a brief respite, grasped her arm and led her away.

At a nod, Robbie slapped the horse's rumps while he discharged his pistol into the air to startle them and occupy the servants' attention while he and Duncan—along with a strangely acquiescent Cairstine slung over his shoulder like a bag of potatoes—made good their escape.

The cattle, unused to such treatment, attempted to rear. The coachman swore, ran to their heads and grabbed the lead horse's bridle. The footman hurried to join him, and they began their struggle to bring the team under control before they broke free from their traces and bolted.

Duncan's and Robbie's own mounts, each tied on a long rein to a sturdy tree, grazed contentedly on the new season greenery and raised uncurious heads to their masters as they returned. Duncan put Cairstine down, untied his horse and swung into the saddle then pulled Cairstine up in front of him. "This will have to do."

She inclined her head. "As you say, sir. Better than shank's pony."

Duncan set his horse to trot as her next words aroused his suspicion that something he had said or done had given away his identity despite his precautions not to do so.

"So, Sir Monk. Am I supposed to be afraid of you?" she asked. "Trembling in my shoes? Or should I, perhaps, be praising you for my deliverance from evil?"

Duncan smiled beneath his mask and answered her by way of slipping his arm around her beautifully slim waist and pulling her closer to his chest.

She smiled. "Ah, a Benedictine with a vow to speak no words, are you?"

He nodded. She swept her curls aside with one hand to display the delicate flesh of her neck. "Maybe I'm a red-haired devil in disguise. One taste and you will be mine."

The urge to nuzzle and kiss nearly overwhelmed him. He shook his head to clear such thoughts from his mind and kicked his horse into a fast canter. Her hair streamed into the breeze at the increase of speed and he smelt violets, even with his nose covered by his mask.

Three hours of hard riding at a pace too fast to permit any further exchange of words to stir his loins brought the bothy he had chosen in view. Duncan dismounted and offered his hands to assist Cairstine down.

She tutted and sprang from the horse's back unaided. "I may have accepted a side-across ride due to not wishing to crease the material of my travelling dress, but as ever, I am quite capable of managing my own descent to the ground."

Duncan heard the words 'as ever' and felt his plan unravelling by the minute, although until she actually named him, she could still answer honestly, if questioned, that she did not know the identity of her abductor. He took her hand to escort her inside the bothy.

She glanced downwards and asked him in a conversational manner, "Did you know the hands of a man of noble birth are smoother than those of one not born so? Even if they are slightly nicked from, let us say…a sporting pastime that involved the releasing of snares."

She pulled her hand from his and walked ahead of him, stiff-backed, into the cottage. He followed her inside. Bread, cheese and a flagon of wine, supplied by Robbie, stood atop of the rough wooden table.

Cairstine looked. "Plain fare but good. Shall I serve the portions, Sir Friar? It is not beneath me to do so, you know."

Duncan stifled a snorted laugh and nodded. She divided the food between three plates and poured wine into thick pottery mugs. He took one of each outside to Robbie, who had unsaddled the horses and stood beside them awaiting further instruction. He handed him his supper and kept his voice low. "The night is warm enough. Will you sleep outside by the bothy door against anyone approaching it overnight?"

Robbie nodded. Duncan returned to Cairstine and found her sat on a three-legged stool eating bread and cheese as if ravenous. She swallowed her mouthful and wiped her lips on the back of her hand. "Do you know how long it has been since I have eaten? Not a bite has passed my lips since I broke my fast this morning with a bowl of watery oatmeal. You forgot that, didn't you?"

He grinned beneath his hood at her outraged expression but did not respond.

Cairstine huffed. "Well, I suppose there's a method to your madness. Do feel free to inform me of it when you will." She set her plate onto the table. "I need the facilities."

Thank the Lord he'd thought of that. Duncan opened the door to what had once been a secure pantry with no window or other way of entering except by the door into the cottage. He'd arranged for a bucket—basic but better than nothing—a bowl of water and a rough cloth. It was the best he could accomplish.

Cairstine looked at it. "Thank you." Then shut the door on him.

Within a few minutes she re-entered the room and walked towards a straw pallet. "This, I suppose, is for me." She yawned. "I presume your man sleeps outside the door on guard for possible intruders. It has been a long day so I will bid you goodnight."

Duncan surveyed her from beneath his hood. Knowing Cairstine as he did, her calm acceptance of her situation was alien to her fiery character, and try as he might he could not bring himself to trust it—or her. However, he thought the rustling of her dress would wake him should she decide during the night to reclothe herself and dispense with his company. He lowered his voice to the strange guttural tone he'd used to make it unrecognizable to her.

"You may. Once you remove your gown."

Cairstine glared at him, arms akimbo and her foot beat out a staccato rhythm on the earth floor. "In your dreams."

*Very likely.*

"Perhaps, but I will control my baser urges, I promise you. However, I can't say I trust you not to leave without saying goodbye. So, it is that or I tie you to the bed. It is your decision."

She narrowed her eyes. "Pass me my blanket."

Duncan threw her the tartan plaid. "I will avert my eyes." He turned his back on her and tried to ignore the rustles he heard. To no avail. Thoughts of what lay beneath her gown stirred his groin and left him relieved to be garbed as a monk with a loose habit to cover the extent of his arousal.

"Here."

Cloth hit him on the head. He lifted her dress from his crown, did his best not to inhale her scent and folded the garment over a stool. "Thank you. Now, my lady, your bed awaits."

"It awaited before you made me disrobe," Cairstine grumbled as she climbed, with the plaid wound around her, onto the pallet. "Men!"

Duncan hid his grin and finished his meal as her breathing became regular and even. With a sigh deep enough to ruffle curtains—had there been any at the window he'd set ajar to refresh the air in the small room—he gazed at her sleeping form. Her lips, the bottom one fuller than the top, were slightly parted, and he longed to kiss them as he lay down on his own pallet close by her.

In the morning, perhaps she would let him? When he apologised for wilfully ruining her reputation so Armstrong would reject her as 'tainted' goods, then fell to his knees to tell her how much he loved her and wanted her to be his wife? He smiled at the thought and drifted off to sleep.

It had been a strange day, Cairstine decided as she settled onto the straw pallet beneath her plaid blanket. She closed her eyes, feigning sleep, which seemed to satisfy her captor as he doused the candle. His cohort, sleeping outside, was snoring so loudly she could hear him even though the door to the bothy was shut. She stifled a giggle then let her mind wander back over the previous few hours.

Neither man had removed their masks and habits, but if either of them were monks, she was a chorus dancer in one of those scandalous shows she as a well-brought-up young lady should not know about. She was fairly sure who one of them was, but had she read those tell-tale signs correctly?

Was she right, and had her talk about the small cuts on his hands told him—as she hoped it had—that she'd guessed his identity and was prepared to go along with whatever he had chosen to do? Weary, as the long day of travel caught up with her, she yawned and drifted off to sleep.

* * * *

It was scarcely light when something woke her. She stayed still. The sound was repeated, and once more she bit back a giggle. Her sleeping companion was restless, and from the small noises he was making she suspected he was having one of 'those' kind of dreams. The type that made you blush when you came to in the morning and remembered it. However, it had served a purpose, for after all she was now wide awake.

A more plentiful supply of water was required than could be found in the ewer provided in the small room, she decided—a small stream or brook would fit the bill nicely. Stealthily she picked up her plaid and folded gown and tiptoed to the window, praying it wouldn't squeak as she carefully eased it wide open. That accomplished, she rolled her dress and blanket into a ball, threw them outside, edged one leg then the other over the sill and scrambled through the opening, grateful for her hoydenish younger years of climbing trees. Then with her chemise decently covered by her plaid blanket, and her gown over her arm, she strode away from the bothy, clear-headed in the brightness of a new day.

As she walked, a small worm of uncertainty wriggled in the pit of her stomach. What if she was she wrong and it wasn't a rescue per se, but something entirely different? Had she wasted an opportunity? Instead of slipping away in search of a good wash, should she have taken the chance to creep up on the sleeping figure and tug his mask from his face? *No, it had to be Duncan.* For surely if the monk had intended to harm her, he would have done so by now? She wished she had the reassurance of having her pistol with her, but Papa had deemed it unnecessary for the journey when their coachmen were armed, so Cairstine had packed it in her trunk.

She shouldn't have listened to him. If it had been in her reticule she could have quickly secured it to her thigh by way of the garter that held her stocking in place when the coach was held up. Still, it was no use repining over the matter now. The riverbed would hopefully provide a largish, suitably rounded stone. Hidden in the pocket of her gown, if the worse came to the worst, she would feign an attempt to unman the monk with her knee once again, then deliver him an eye-watering surprise by way of smashing the rock into his groin with the full force of her arm.

Somewhat reassured to have a plan of action in place, she walked on until she heard the sweet music of a babbling brook. A tiny burn came into view and once she reached it, she unfolded her gown and shook it vigorously. Sad to say, it would never be the same again. However, she draped it over the branch of a convenient tree, wrapped in the plaid blanket—thankfully clean and sweet-smelling—and headed for the water to immerse herself to ready to face whatever challenges the day ahead had in store for her.

She hoped.

The water was peaty in colour – it must come from the hills nearby – but otherwise clear. Cairstine sniffed. It smelled fresh. She decided to take a chance, cupped her hands together to take a drink and, once her thirst was quenched, looked around with caution.

No one to be seen.

It might go against the grain of many of her contemporaries, but cold burn water was better than not washing. She flung the blanket to one side, pulled her chemise over her head and stepped into the water. Although it was in the main only inches deep, a short incline a few yards away meant the water flowed faster and created a tiny pool where the water came to her calves.

Cairstine sank down on her knees and splashed water all over herself. The water was cold but at least it had lost some of the iciness it would have had a few months before.

The sun rose steadily over the horizon in front of her, and its soft warmth was a balm to her chilly skin. Even so she saw no need to linger so as soon as she felt clean, she stood up, stretched for the blanket and wound it around her torso. It would double as a towel as well as covering her. Once dry she would redress, head back to the cottage and no doubt face the wrath of her captor.

Warm again, Cairstine rested one foot on the bank, ready to step out of the burn.

"What the blazes do you think you are doing, woman?"

The familiar voice was so unexpected, she tripped.

Cairstine accepted that without a shadow of a doubt she was going to end up in the water again. She swayed, flailed her arms and tried to stay upright.

The blanket began to unwind. She grabbed the sides and shut her eyes.

*How embarrassing.*

She felt a strong arm around her waist before her feet lifted and she was swung through the air.

"I've got you. Don't worry, your blushes are spared. The tanning I'd like to give you for wandering off is held in abeyance. What on earth were you up to?" She was dropped inelegantly onto terra firma. "Are you trying to annoy me?"

"A call of nature and a wash." Cairstine glared at her captor. "You and your henchman were in the arms of Morpheus. I had hoped to return without you knowing."

"You were going to return?"

That he'd forgotten to disguise his voice in the heat of the moment made Cairstine smile. She was tempted to let him play it his way for a little longer. In a strange manner it was both exhilarating and exciting. While the charade played out she could pretend that things were very different to what they were.

Nevertheless, the time for performing was over. Corbridge had to be reached without delay and if Duncan really was determined to help her they needed to plot.

"Of course I was. Now, for goodness' sake, Duncan. Remove that idiotic robe and mask. I need you to help me find a blasted letter."

# Chapter Four

Duncan pulled off his monk's garb and untied his mask. He essayed a rueful grin. "I forgot to disguise my voice, didn't I?"

Cairstine tutted and raised her eyes heavenward. "Do feel free to explain just what has led you to believe I have become suddenly stupid and easily fooled since we last met? As well as that, there was also the condition of your hands. And the way you hold yourself when you walk. Let alone we have ridden together often enough that I know how you seat yourself in the saddle when mounted."

He held his hands up in mock surrender. "Yes. Yes. I should have known better. But give over now, woman. I meant it for the best. Come sit beside me and tell me what is going on. I will turn my back while you dress."

She tapped her foot and looked at him with narrowed eyes. "Hmmm… Well, I will. For retrieving this letter is of the utmost importance. However, you will give me a full account of your actions when I have done so." The words 'or else it will be the worse for you' were intimated, if not spoken.

Duncan looked at the determined gleam in the green of her eyes and smiled. "Yes, my l…" He stuttered then choked down the word on the tip of his tongue. Cairstine was not his 'love' yet, much as he wished it otherwise. He swung around and faced away from her.

The enticing rustle of her clothes filled his ears. With difficulty, he diverted his mind away from the glimpse of white thigh and pert buttock that had caught his eye when she'd nearly fallen into the burn by silently reciting the alphabet forwards then backwards until she announced, "I am ready."

He turned and saw her sat by the rippling water, the plaid blanket hung on a tree branch to dry. She patted the ground to her side.

"It is such a mess," she told him as he sat down. "A real stramash. Papa is at his wit's end."

Duncan listened with growing concern as Cairstine related the circumstances surrounding the letter and exhaled loudly when she finished.

"I agree with your father. If made public, the letter spells ruin for your family. We must retrieve it and turn it to ash so it can never threaten you again."

Cairstine rested her chin on her curled hand and gazed pensively into the distance. "I was intending to play along with the marriage plans while inventing small excuses to delay it actually taking place while I searched. It was the best idea I could come up with,"

Duncan frowned. "I dislike the thought of you staying in Armstrong's house alone, under his power, so to speak."

"Not alone. My papa would have been there."

His worry lines deepened. "With the best will in the world, I don't believe your father's presence would have aided you. He doesn't appear to be thinking clearly. It seems to me as if this situation has taken possession of his mind so thoroughly, he cannot envisage any way out of this morass other than the obvious one of you marrying Armstrong."

Cairstine bit her lip, her expression unsure, as if his words did not sit well—or maybe didn't fit her own image of the man that was her father. "I suppose so… Or Papa may have had a plan of his own to stop the marriage and just not confided it to me."

Given Cairstine's close relationship with her parent, Duncan agreed. "That could be the case. When all is said and done you are still his child…and a daughter at that. He's been forced to embroil you in this matter, but his instinct will be to shield you when possible."

He regretted his words as soon as they were out of his mouth. Cairstine's eyes flashed fire. If she'd been standing, she would have surely stamped her foot. "You men! I am *not* a child, nor incapable for being female. It's *my* future at stake here. Enough is enough. Going forwards my destiny will be my own to decide."

Duncan thought quickly. If he wasn't careful Cairstine would be flouncing off without him again. He nudged her shoulder with his then gave her a sideways glance like he used to when daring her to join him in some piece of mischief when they were young. "So, what are we going to do?"

"*I* am going to Corbridge—"

In the absence of a pigtail, he gave a tress of her hair a sharp tug. "Pack it in, brat. *We* are going to Corbridge."

Her eyes watered. "Ouch. Duncan!" She punched his upper arm. Hard. Then, as it had ever been, they were back on good terms once more.

"We need to come up with a reason why I am accompanying you in his place…"

Cairstine nodded and an idea occurred to him.

"How about your papa was taken ill on the road leaving you with no choice but to return home for a fresh escort in the form of me? There can be no disguising my dislike of Armstrong. I've always been outspoken on the subject of his boorish ways. But if I maintain the façade of the bored indifference of a man labouring under an obligation to a near neighbour, I believe I could get him to invite me to stay the night."

She bit her lip. "Just one night…"

He smiled. "We should not need more if we both play our part, although I will not be leaving without you no matter whether our ploy is successful or not."

She returned his smile and he saw the playful sparkle return to her eyes. "So, Sir Fake Friar. How do you suggest we act out this cunning charade?"

Duncan grinned. "That to go along with my boredom over the chore of escorting you south, I regard you in the light of an irritating younger sister I am happy to get off my hands. While you are going to be as silly and giddy as any Bath Miss. Happy and excited to be the bride of a man who would go to such lengths to obtain your hand."

She snorted, then giggled. "That will take some doing. I'd much rather scratch his eyes out."

He laughed. "I know, but I am wagering he does not. After all, you haven't mixed in the same circles and I'd guess any gossip of you would be quite tame?"

"More than likely. As I'm not officially out yet, I have always been mindful of the sensibilities and necessity of appearing meek and demure. I would not receive my voucher for Almack's otherwise."

Duncan raised one eyebrow and she laughed.

"Well, tried to," she temporized. "Generally, I think I succeeded. After all, I rarely appear anywhere the ton is, not yet. Therefore it is easy to be my true self and to run free at home. Papa might shake his head, but he does little or nothing to curb me. So yes, go on, what else?"

"As I'd much rather call him out for his devious dealings, and will do so if it becomes necessary, I think we—"

"Duncan." She put her hands on her hips and glared at him. "No. I won't have you risk your life on my behalf."

*I could and I would.*

He smiled reassuringly and circled that particular reply. "It will not come to that, I think. If he perceives no threat from me and you flirt very prettily your admiration of what he has done, between us we can ply him with enough drink over dinner to loosen his tongue."

Cairstine squared her shoulders. "I shall do so and not give away that I'd rather vomit."

Duncan nodded. "And what of your papa? What action will he have taken when I whisked you away? Returned home to send out a search party?"

She bit her lip. "I'm not sure, but he will have sent out a search party at the very least, I think."

"I never intended to discomfort him for more than a day or two before I took you home. We could leave them to fruitlessly search while we head off to

Corbridge, but that wouldn't be fair to the men, or your father."

"I'm not running tamely home like some feeble milk-and-water young miss. We'll be sticking to the plan we've just devised between us."

"Then we must soothe your father's fears without disclosing our true intentions and give him no urgent reason to head south again. We can send him a message by way of Robbie to reassure him that we have matters well in hand. Tell him I happened to come across two villains absconding with you, dealt with them and am now seeing you safely to Armstrong's. That you will write to him when you arrive, etcetera, blah, blah."

Cairstine agreed. "If nothing else, it will assure him he has no immediate need to rush post-haste to Corbridge to be at my side, and with a head start we can accomplish what we've set out to do." She fixed him with a steely-eyed stare. "So, it's Robbie Logan you have with you, is it? I should have guessed. Now explain yourself, Duncan Callander. What on earth did you think you were about?"

He was not a man given to blushing, but he felt the heat rise on his cheeks as he admitted, "Before I knew about the letter, I thought it was the smaller matter of making Armstrong not wish to marry you..."

"So you thought to ruin my reputation so he would reject me as spoiled goods?"

His colour deepened. "Well, yes. And I disguised myself so you could answer with honesty, even on the Bible if necessary, that you didn't know your kidnapper."

Her eyes flashed their warning that her temper was on the rise. He bit back a grin. This was not the time to show how much he loved that feisty side of her.

"Oh, how considerate of you." She rolled said eyes. "At no point did it occur to you that as well as Armstrong, what you have done means no other man will wish to marry me either?"

His heart thumped inside his chest as he met her gaze. He had to answer her honestly and hope she didn't reward him with a black eye, or worse. "I do. I've wanted to ask you to be my wife for months now but held back for you to have your debut Season in London."

"Which was a waste of time for I will not now be having one."

He pulled her hand to his lips and kissed the back of it. "Play fair, my prickly love. That option was no longer on the cards from the moment Armstrong showed his hand. But when we are wed, we could take a house in Edinburgh and join the social whirl there for a few weeks if you'd like to."

Duncan held his breath. One day he would, he vowed, do the correct thing and formally ask for her hand in marriage.

"Oh, I'm your love and we're to be wed, are we? Are you sure you're not presuming too much?" She stuck her chin out in a way he recognised. Cairstine was about to be stubborn for the sake of it.

He tilted said chin with his fingertips and held her gaze. "I don't know. Am I?"

Cairstine huffed but Duncan saw a brief glint of mischief light her eyes. "I can't say I've decided as yet, but as I'm now a fallen woman by your doing, you should kiss me. It may help me make up my mind until you do ask me properly."

Duncan needed no further prompting. He cupped the back of her head and urged her closer. Her lips parted and he deepened their kiss, his heart beating harder when her response was neither hesitant nor shy. As she threaded her fingers through the back of his hair, the gentle tugs he thought she was unaware of making notched up his arousal. Her breasts pressed against his chest and he would swear her nipples were as hard and as tight as his were. Her breath was as harsh and uneven as he moved his lips to the soft skin beneath her ear. "So…?"

"Hmm… Maybe… Or maybe I shall need more kisses before I decide." She raised her eyebrows. "Practice is always needed."

He grinned and administered a sharp smack on her rear. "Away with you, you minx. Back to the bothy at once before you heat my blood past bearing."

She giggled, jumped to her feet and snatched the plaid from the branch as she darted away, her long red curls streaming behind her as she picked up speed. "Race you—"

Cairstine heard Duncan's footfalls pounding behind her and squealed when his arm snaked around her waist, halting her flight. Her feet left the ground and he swung her around and around. "Ha. Caught you…even though you set off without me."

She laughed as he steadied her return to the ground. "I needed to. You should try running with several layers of material flapping around your legs."

He looked revolted at the thought. "No, thank you. Trying to walk while wearing the monk's habit was quite bad enough."

She giggled, threaded her arm through his and they walked to the cottage, whistling the silly marching tunes of their youth. As they reached it, the door opened and Robbie walked out. He looked at Duncan and lifted his own cowl and mask.

"M'lord...everything is well? I became afeart when I heard no sound from within and opened the door to find you and ma lady no inside."

Cairstine had always had a soft spot for Robbie, knowing him to be as loyal to Duncan as his father, Bruce, had been to Duncan's elder brother, so she apologised. How on earth she hadn't realised Duncan's companion was he she had no idea. "I'm sorry, Robbie. It was my fault. I couldn't find anything on which to write a note to let Duncan know I'd slipped outside to...ah...um...freshen up. He came in search of me."

Robbie blushed as if he recognised the euphemism—as she'd intended he should by her hesitation. "Ah, weel, aye, but I was afeart for both of ye."

She smiled. "And I thank you for being so."

Duncan coughed. "So, niceties completed, may we get on?"

Cairstine swept him the full court curtsey she had been practicing for her Presentation to their Majesties—or the Prince Regent and his sister, Princess Sophia, if they were standing in for his poor, mad father, King George. "As you wish, my lord."

Duncan grinned. "Very lovely...given your stained and travel-worn dress."

She placed her hand on her hip and glared at him, although a smile still played at the corners of her lips. "And whose fault is that, pray?"

He held up his hands. "I will own it and you may take me to task when I have seen Robbie on his way."

She took his hint and nodded. "If by any chance my travelling portmanteau could be bought back when

Robbie delivers the message to my father, I will be able to mend my sad appearance. I do not choose to appear like a hoyden." She grinned. "Not most of the time, anyway. Meanwhile, I saw a likely spot on my way to the burn, so I'm away to forage mushrooms and watercress for our breakfast."

She walked off and heard Duncan explain what else was needed to Robbie. "Harness and bring my curricle. Explain to His Grace we are travelling light to make up lost time. Lady McColl will write him of her safe arrival once she has reached her destination. Come. I will tell you the rest of the taradiddle you are to relay to him while you saddle up." His voice faded away as she continued to walk in the direction she hoped was the correct one. How ignominious if she had to retrace her steps and admit failure.

She lost sight of the men as the ground became wet and spongy underfoot and she re-lived Duncan's kiss as she bent to pluck the first mushroom. It had thrilled her in a positively un-maidenly way that had left her wanting more, although she was uncertain how much 'more' actually was. Definitely more kisses, and the touch of his hand on her skin in the places that tingled with the anticipation of him doing so. To find some undergrowth or a tree in the way she had noticed other couples do?

It just did not sound comfortable. A bed though? Her heart beat faster. He'd called her 'my love', albeit a 'prickly' one, and he wanted to marry her.

Cairstine pictured it and smiled as her good fortune dawned on her. Childhood friendship had blossomed into love between a man and a woman. Her proposed union with Armstrong might revolt her, but it was far from unusual for females of her rank to be married to suit dynastic ambition and the accumulation of wealth.

That brought Armstrong to mind. She shivered. Nothing was yet certain. There was still the letter to find, but on one point she was determined—she would give her virginity to the man she loved, not George. Bloody. Armstrong.

Duncan called her name and she refocused her attention on the matter at hand. She glanced towards her lap and found it full of plump field mushrooms, the watercress by her feet.

"Over here. What have you got?"

A brace of trout held by their tails dangled from his hand when he came into view. "I have guddled us a pair. Let's go back to the bothy and cook a breakfast picnic. I'm starving."

She smiled, plucked at her skirt to form a pocket to carry her harvest and stood. "So you have. If you gut them, I will heat the pan and prepare the mushrooms and watercress." The peppery flavour of the herb would work well with the fish.

She left him whistling outside while he prepared the fish and walked into the cottage to do her part. Less than half an hour later the sizzling fish had released enough oil for her to add the cleaned mushrooms and herbs. Duncan sniffed hungrily as she spooned the contents of the pan onto their plates. "Oh, that smells good. I confess I hadn't realised how hungry I was until you started to cook. My stomach has been rumbling ever since."

Cairstine smiled. "A slightly odd combination to be eating for a breakfast, but beggars can't be choosers."

"Nothing is an odd combination when you're ready for food as I am."

Her stomach chose to emulate his and she giggled. "And me."

For several minutes the only sounds were of food being eaten and plates being scraped until at last both put their knives down and sighed.

"A feast," Cairstine said. "A veritable banquet. I have never enjoyed a meal more."

"Nor I. Let me dispose of the bones where some animal or raptor will no doubt appreciate them and wash the plates in the burn."

Cairstine nodded, and as soon as he'd gone did her best to tidy her appearance. She was attempting to untangle her curls with her fingertips when he returned, came up behind her and pressed his lips into her hair. It felt entirely natural to turn into his arms and tilt her face up for his kiss.

# Chapter Five

Duncan buried his face in Cairstine's pretty red curls and she turned towards him, her eyes closed and lips parted. He bent his face to hers and their tongues entwined. The touch of her fingers as she explored the contours of his back through the material of his fine linen shirt was instantly arousing. Despite his best intentions, his cock responded to her touch and he scolded himself. *Not so fast.* He had to force himself to remember here was a well-brought-up young lady. No hoyden or forwards miss who knew all the unspoken rules of seduction and acquiesced to them. With an unuttered oath hovering on his lips, Duncan attempted to widen the gap between them so she would not feel his stiffening erection.

It wasn't as easy as he'd hoped. Cairstine moaned, soft, soulful and full of pent-up emotion, kissed him harder and moved her hand. Her fingertips brushed lightly over the bulge in his buckskins.

*Oh, sweet lord.* Duncan groaned when his shaft fully hardened and attempted to burst free from the confines of the material.

"Stop now, sweetheart…"

Her touch on his groin became firmer and she ran her fingers over the outline of his shaft. "And if I don't wish to?" Her voice was husky with desire. "What will you do?"

How could he respond to that?

Duncan willed his unruly staff to behave for a few moments more and gazed into her eyes. "Are you sure, my love?" If she said no he'd have no option but to leave her presence and sort himself out. So less satisfying and, the way he felt at that moment, almost cheating.

She looked at him, her eyes calm, full of trust. "I've never been surer." As if to confirm her choice, she began to loosen the neck of his shirt, then the adorable hint of mischief he knew and loved returned to her eyes. "I presume this is the point where we remove our clothes? I'm not exactly sure of the niceties so I do hope you're ready to lead the way and guide me."

Relief poured through Duncan and he smiled in remembrance of the sights they had both seen over the years. Cairstine was a virgin but she was not totally naive. "It's not strictly necessary to be naked, as you know. I could free my manhood and tip up your skirt…but I would prefer to make love to you naked. Skin to skin. Every part of us given to each other. If you would like that too?"

She tugged at his shirt. "Oh, yes. I think I would like that very much indeed."

He kissed her lips. "Wait here, sweetheart. I'll lay the plaid over our bed. The pallet is scratchy." Duncan covered the straw pallet with the softer blanket, considered it was the best he could do in the circumstances, and took a deep breath. This was it, something he had long hoped for and wondered if the time would ever come.

"My lady, our bed awaits." The bow he added was everything a bow should be.

Cairstine laughed, curtseyed then unfastened the tiny buttons down the front of her dress as she walked towards him. When she reached his side, she shrugged the gown off so it pooled at her feet. "My lord, I am yours."

His heart beat harder at the sight of the round moons of her breasts rising above the scooped neckline of her chemise.

Without taking his eyes off her, Duncan removed his shirt, lay down and raised one eyebrow. "Will you join me?"

Cairstine laughed somewhat breathlessly as she did as he bade her. "It will be my pleasure."

Her warm body moulded to his side as if they had lain like that for years. Duncan considered how it felt. The only answer he could come up with was 'as it should be'. He bent his head and kissed her, long and deep, while untying the silken ribbons that closed the front of her undergarment. He continued to nibble and kiss along her neck before he eased her chemise over her shoulders and down her body. His breathing deepened at the sight of her breasts, pert and round with rose-pink nipples. "Perfect." He stroked his fingertips over them and revelled at her indrawn breath as they puckered at his touch.

The nubs hardened and the throb of his cock built as he teased them gently with his tongue. A small, kittenish mewl escaped her and she knotted her fingers through the back of his hair to the point of pain. He sucked harder on one bud then the other and pushed the remainder of her undergarments over her thighs so Cairstine could free her legs from them.

He gazed at her naked perfection—the golden triangle between her legs, the creamy soft flesh of her thighs.

"So beautiful…"

"I need to be able to say the same thing."

She tugged on his trousers. He shrugged them off. His cock sprang free and her eyes widened slightly as if the knowledge had just come to her as to which bit of each of them fitted where. Still, she didn't hesitate and reached for his shaft. The pulse of his cock increased as she grasped it, his balls full and heavy beneath it.

He stroked between her legs and found her wet and ready, slid a finger inside her and added another. She lifted her hips to welcome his touch, so he lay over her and eased in his cockhead. Her breathing became faster as he pushed his shaft deeper until he felt a point of resistance that, with a quick thrust, he moved past, and claimed her for his own. Her breath hitched with a small squeak, so he stilled and kissed her lips.

"You're mine now, my love, as I am yours."

She sighed and moved against him. "Yes."

With a brief nod of thanks towards the experienced matron who had initiated him into the art, he moved his cock gently and slowly inside her until she began to pant. Then he gave in to his need to thrust harder and she responded, meeting his rhythm until he heard her soft whisper.

"Oh…oh…oh…yes."

He increased his pace as she writhed beneath him, and groaned his climax when his seed released, then he stilled and held her close until their breathing steadied. She kissed his neck. He withdrew and rolled to his side. She laid her head on his chest. He stroked down the length of her back, relaxed, and a way forwards came to him. He lent up on his elbow and smiled. "So, that's us well and truly compromised. Our social standing now lies in tatters."

Cairstine gazed at him. "Why do you look rather happy about that?" Her eyes widened and her expression changed as she realised the probable cause. "You've thought of something, haven't you?"

He nodded. "I think we should handfast. When Robbie returns he can bear witness and listen to our vows. At least then we are wed here if not south of the border. Our formal marriage ceremony at the kirk can take place once we have dealt with Armstrong."

She smiled her agreement then teased him.

"As long as I receive my portmanteau containing my fresh dress and comb. It would not be seemly for the daughter of a duke to become the Countess of Callander while appearing crumpled."

Pinning her hands above her head and kissing her lips. "Admit it. You would marry me barefoot dressed only in your petticoat as I would you clothed in only this blanket.

"Cocky." She chuckled and kissed him back. "Yes, I would, but now let me up. Robbie will be back soon."

He glanced ruefully down at his rapidly softening shaft. "A pity."

* * * *

Cairstine washed hurriedly in the basin of lukewarm water Duncan had put on the table before he'd thoughtfully left her for a few moments to allow her to do what she had to. His comment that if they'd had more time he would have gladly performed that task had made her blush.

He'd laughed. "*You'll soon get used to my intentions to make life as perfect for you as I can. I promise to always say what I mean, what I desire and what I would like. I also promise to listen to your needs and desires and when possible make them happen.*" He'd kissed her nose. "*My vows continue. I will never ever do something you do not want. We, my love, are partners. Something not common between man and wife, but why be common?*"

That was a statement to agree with and be happy about. The state of her gown, however, was not. Even with a good shake and dust down, it still looked…disreputable, she decided. As if she'd been rolling around in the hay.

Which, she thought, wasn't too far from the truth. Nevertheless, if Robbie turned up trumps and brought her portmanteau, she would be able to dress in an appropriate manner for whatever the day threw at her.

*Handfasting?* Her heart quickened. If, over the years she had dreamed that one day she and Duncan would become a couple, she'd forced those nebulous thoughts to the back of her mind. To handfast might not be legal south of the border, but that was Sassenachs for you. In her homeland it was. Once they ventured into England it might not give her the protection it would in Scotland, but if nothing else, the thought of illegality if she wed again might give any suitor pause for thought.

Hopefully that would include Armstrong.

Cairstine looked around the cottage and the practical side of her nature decided a little tidying was required. Whether they spent any more time there or not, there was no reason to be messy, and if the place was orderly, it would be so much easier to find things. For one, she was sure a country dwelling like this should have a store of root vegetables somewhere. Whatever Robbie had or hadn't managed to bring with him, if it could be supplemented there would be one less meal to worry about. As she had no idea how long they would stop at the bothy, or even how many of them would, she'd rather err on the side of more rather than less.

A tuneful whistle heralded the return of Duncan.

"All clear?"

"All clear," she replied with a laugh. "I'm as decent as I can be with crumpled clothing and no hairbrush."

"Me too. I've asked Robbie to bring my shaving gear as well as a change of clothes." Duncan re-entered the bothy scratching the dark shadow on his jawline, and grinned. "You are far too dressed for my liking. I much prefer you naked."

Cairstine's cheeks heated at the thought of how much she'd enjoyed them both being so. "Well, yes," she mumbled. "And I you, but for now we are as we must be. When do you expect Robbie back?"

Duncan shrugged. "Before dusk. It depends on if he had to wait for your father to receive him and how easily he was able to get hold of what we need. For now, I've the happy news that when I sent him on his way this morning, I asked him to set snares if he caught sight of a warren, and one of them has borne fruit. Well, not fruit, but a rabbit. I've skinned and jointed it, so we could maybe have a rabbit stew for supper if he returns too late in the day for us to set out for Armstrong's place?" He opened an oilskin and put it and the contents on the scrubbed table.

"Then we need some vegetables," Cairstine stated. "Does the cottage have a root cellar?"

Duncan nodded. "At the stable end. I'll go and discover what's lurking in there."

She rather hoped for something more appealingly palatable than the word *lurking* seemed to suggest and cleaned her knife while she waited. Not five minutes later Duncan reappeared with, thankfully, fresh, not mouldy basics Cook had taught her to prepare. Neeps of course. Neeps—turnips—were a staple of any Scotsman's diet, which along with the tatties and carrots he carried could be the basis of many a meal.

Duncan offered them to her. "Can you do something with these?"

"Of course." Any Scotswoman worth her salt—an expensive commodity—could, be she a commoner or aristocrat. It wasn't that long ago starvation had stared most Scots in the face. In the south the Reivers had raided and driven off their livestock with no regard to any cultivated land their horses trampled down in the process. Farther north the clearances had caused untold hardships. How landlords could order their tenants off the land with no thought of how they would cope was something Cairstine couldn't comprehend. To her it went against all precepts of decency.

Cairstine began to scrub the vegetables. "This is when I thank my mama for encouraging me to spend time in the kitchen with Cook. Papa was horrified, but Mama said that although the Reivers hadn't raided in her lifetime, they had in her mother's and that the Laird and his lady had best be prepared for the influx of the young, weak and elderly that would seek refuge behind their fortified walls."

"While the men were away trying to recover what had been taken?" Duncan suggested.

Cairstine remembered Cook's hissed confidences. *"Even the strongest of lasses stood no chance if caught by the tail end of the raiding party while their menfolk were chasing after the main herd. Pinned down as each of them took her in turn, many did not survive the ordeal. Behind the castle walls was where you needed to be if you were in any way bonnie, even if that meant you existed on nettle and neep soup."*

"Just so."

Duncan hovered behind her. "Do I need to do anything?"

She rolled her eyes. Said exactly like a man who hoped the answer would be a categorical 'no'. She chose to tease him.

"Yes."

He paled. "I do?"

Cairstine put him out of his misery. "Yes. Go away and leave a woman to do what must be done. See if there is anything else that could be of use?"

He placed his hands on her shoulders and kissed her neck. She turned and flapped her hands at him.

"You are a severe distraction, my lord. Off with you. Go keep watch for Robbie and let me accomplish my tasks in peace."

He smacked her arse. "I will, with every expectation of enjoying the fruits of your labour later."

Cairstine squealed and rubbed her rear with a very exaggerated gesture. "My lord. I declare you are not a gentleman. That was quite unexpected." It stung, although not as much as she intimated.

"Be that as it may, my lady, I believe you enjoyed it all the same?"

Cairstine giggled and bit the end of his nose. "So I did, but do not expect me to acquiesce without a fight."

Duncan chuckled and rubbed his nose. "I look forward to our bouts, my love, but in the meantime, I will feed and water our remaining mount against our need to ride two-up should any circumstance prevent Robbie's return."

Without Duncan around to distract her it only took a few moments to slice and cut the vegetables, add the few wild herbs and a couple of mushrooms left over from their breakfast and set them to boil, sear the rabbit, then to amalgamate them in the big pot she had found. The aroma made her tummy grumble, although truth be told she wasn't yet truly hungry. Her unusual breakfast had filled her. With nothing more to be done while the stew bubbled, she gave the pot a last stir then plumped up the straw pallet, shook out the blanket and surveyed the result. The bed, if not inviting, looked sleepable on.

*And the rest.*

Her body tensed, her nipples hardened and her nether regions pulsed as she remembered just what 'the rest' entailed before she blushed. *Scratchy straw be damned. Duncan spread the dark-coloured plaid so the loss of my maidenhead would not seep into flaxen-coloured stalks to require their being disposed of – with every possibility of Robbie's raised eyebrows on why burning a quantity of my bed might be necessary.*

*Enough.* Sadly, getting hot and bothered would not help her situation at that moment. Cairstine strove to think of other things.

What she would have liked to have had to hand was the novel she'd been reading in the carriage before her abduction. She was at an exciting point in the story, and if nothing else it would have passed a few pleasant minutes. Cairstine gazed around the room and noticed the tome on a shelf, next to a Holy Bible and a couple of well-thumbed books. Eschewing *Leonora* by Mari Edgeworth, for after all she had read it many times, she opened *Waverley*.

When someone tapped her on the shoulder she jumped and shrieked. "Whaaa..."

"Grief, lassie, ah mean, ma lady..." Robbie walked around to face her. "I thought you were asleep and I needed to wake you. I spoke to you and ye ignored me."

"Sorry, Robbie. I was engrossed." She scanned the room. "Have you seen Duncan?"

"He's on his way with some more parcels from the wagon."

"The wagon...?"

"I thought it be better than his lordship's curricle. Less to notice and be nebby aboot. You sit up high in yon contraption, eh? Dressed as a lord and lady should be, ye'll attract the kind o' notice ye are anxious to avoid. Your faces are weel-known aroond these parts, ye ken fine weel and beggin' yoor pardon, ma lady, yoor presence, unchaperoned, will attract an awfy lot o' comment. I've taken the liberty o' poaching a few homespun garments from the servants' washing line."

"Well reasoned," Cairstine said in admiration. "After all, any number of farmers could be about with a wagon full of parcels and packages. As for nebby—nosiness—this should help perfectly."

"Mind tho," Duncan added as he shouldered his way into the bothy, "we mun restoor oor appearance afore we reach Armstrong's hoose if I am to be invited in to play my part." He grinned. "Hence my practicing my accent so if need be I can switch to it without thinking. Robbie will take my horse home and catch us up on the road to Carlisle in my curricle so we may make the change."

"Oh?" Her interest was piqued along with her enjoyment of the ability to tease Duncan whenever she could. "How shall we present ourselves, my lord? Shall we be itinerant workers looking for employment? Or perhaps a married couple travelling to the big city to try our luck? Do tell."

Duncan grinned with an airy flick of his hand. "We shall be a curate and his wife, down on our beam ends for reasons too sensitive to divulge."

"The vicar made overtures to the wife," Cairstine added with a giggle. "Which outraged the curate, who planted a facer on the vicar, who immediately complained to the bishop and threatened all sorts of dire things if the curate was not removed immediately."

"A vivid imagination is a wonderful thing." Duncan snorted. "I like it. Anything else?"

"When the vicar was in his cups, he boasted the woman would be his, willing or not. The curate didn't wait to find out whether that was about to happen but collected their belongings and they stole out in the middle of the night. Bartered for the wagon from a local farmer and are on the way to…to…oh, somewhere. That bit can be your idea."

Duncan rolled his eyes. "Thank you. Let's hope it isn't needed. My imagination is not as productive as yours, I fear."

Robbie ignored their chit-chat and sniffed. "Is that rabbit stew? I've not eaten for so long, I'm fair clemmed."

Cairstine smiled. "It is indeed. Sit at the table, and if you have brought bread from home, carve the loaf, please?"

Robbie blushed. "I cannae eat at the same board as ye, lass. You being the daughter of a duke an' all."

Cairstine turned to the pot and stirred. "Rubbish." She pointed the spoon at him. Stock dripped off it and she hastily put it back into the pot. There wasn't enough to waste even one drip. "You can and will sit with us. I'm as clemmed as you and would prefer not to wait until after we have dined to hear your report of what my papa said."

Robbie nodded his acceptance and took a wrapped loaf from the pile of parcels Duncan had carried into the bothy. "I had to get what I could without showing myself too much. My da was a good help, and he's all ready to make sure he covers for you as best he can."

Duncan pulled back a chair and sat. "And His Grace…?"

"Wasnae so easy to calm doon. Fair on his high horsie at first. But, once he thought aboot it, he said he would do as Duncan advised. Anywauh, he's puttin it aboot you're no weel." The more excited he got the thicker the accent. "Whit noo?"

Cairstine ladled stew into earthenware bowls, set them down on the table and took her own place.

"First, we eat." Duncan took Cairstine's hand. "Then you listen to our vows as we handfast."

Robbie's mouth dropped open. "Ah, *me*?"

Cairstine nodded and touched him on the shoulder. "Please," she beseeched him. "Your father served Fraser above the call of duty as you serve Duncan. There could be no one better."

The fresh blush that spread over his cheeks was endearing. She gave into impulse and hugged him. Not the sort of thing most aristocrats would do with a servant, but she'd long decided she would act as *she* thought fit, not as society decreed. It made for a much more comfortable life at present.

"I agree with my lady here." Duncan added his mite as he spooned up the last of his supper. "We want someone who is important to our clans to stand for us. Will you?"

"Aye, of course." Robbie squared his shoulders. "Whaur de ye fancy tae dae it?"

"By the stream," Cairstine said with a slight blush of her own when Duncan grinned and she remembered her plaid wrapping parting when she'd lost her footing. "If you men would give me a few moments to tidy myself?"

Robbie went even redder, if that was possible. "I'll wait ootside."

Duncan winked. "Don't forget to shout if you need any help in dressing."

Cairstine waggled her finger at him. The man was incorrigible. And she loved it.

*Loved?* She thought for a moment. *Yes, loved.*

"I'm sure I'll manage."

# Chapter Six

The door closed behind them and she rummaged in the travelling portmanteau that Robbie had retrieved from home and Duncan had brought into the bothy. Inside was the muslin gown, carefully folded by her maid in the expectation that she would wish to exchange her travelling gown to eat dinner with her papa at the inn. To her current delight, she had not managed to summon the energy to do so and it was still pristine, as was the fine lace shawl that would be looked down on by no one—let alone an Armstrong. Her dressing case held her hairbrush and pins, a piece of soap and, most wonderful of all, her toothbrush, a small tin of Brown's Cleansing Powder and a vial of her precious violet perfume.

The pitcher was still half-full, and although the water was in no way warm, Cairstine was more than happy to strip off and use it for the pleasure of feeling properly clean. Her hair she brushed and left loose, then she re-dressed, added a dab of perfume and draped her shawl around her shoulders. She stepped outside and saw Duncan had used the time to mend his own appearance with an even chillier wash and shave in the burn. He and Robbie sat side by side on a convenient fallen tree a few yards away.

When Duncan saw her, he stood and kicked Robbie, who followed suit.

"My lady, will you do me the honour of a handfast?"

She curtseyed. "It will be my pleasure."

He bowed. "As it will be mine."

Duncan took in the scene as he straightened and thought if perfect. The sun shone, somewhere a robin chirruped and high above a buzzard called. The stream danced and rippled, and the atmosphere was both peaceful and arousing. Robbie looked at him.

"Will ye hold hands with your lady and say your words of commitment to her?"

Duncan smiled and took her hand. "My lovely Cairstine, my one true love for now and ever, will you be mine as I promise to be yours, forever? I will love you, protect you and share with you all I have for as long as I live."

She gulped. *How perfect.* Then answered. "I will, my lord. And this is my solemn vow. Duncan, I will love you, be true to you and be yours for as long as I live."

Robbie sighed. "Aww, that's braw. I noo pronounce you to be handfast. Er, mebbee a wee kiss?"

Cairstine smiled as Duncan leant closer, pecked her lips and whispered, "I'll follow that up later when I've sent Robbie on his way."

She could hardly wait.

* * * *

Duncan released his bride with reluctance and turned towards Robbie—the Sassenachs could think what they liked but as far as he was concerned, Cairstine was now his wife and he wanted no other person in earshot of their wedding night. He ignored a twinge of guilt for requiring Robbie to make the same journey twice in one day. "Still, we may need my curricle to enable us arrive at our destination in finer style. Given the time of year, several hours of daylight remain. On horseback you will reach home before dark if you set out now. Cairstine and I will leave in the wagon at daybreak."

Robbie nodded, a knowing twinkle lighting his eye. "Aye, mebbee that'd be best. I'll saddle up and be on my way. The homespun garments are in the largest parcel."

Duncan reached into his pocket and tossed him a golden guinea. "The Bay Horse at West Woodburn is around sixteen miles from our destination. It's a tad far from our journey's end, I admit, but I would prefer us not to be too close to Corbridge. Best to not be seen and remembered. Put up there until we catch up with you."

Robbie caught the coin and walked away. Duncan tugged Cairstine back into his arms. "Now, where were we…?"

She gazed into his eyes and held her breath. He didn't kiss her, but instead grasped her waist and threw her over his shoulder with a firm smack on her arse. "Yes. This is it."

Cairstine giggled and pummelled his back. "Duncan Callander! Put me down at once, you wretch. You will have this dress in the same state as my travelling gown."

Duncan laughed and strode towards the bothy. "It will cease to be a nuisance soon, for you will not be wearing it shortly, my love."

She giggled as he carried her over the threshold and set her down. "In no way a castle or a manor house, I'm afraid," he said. "We can arrange a rather grander affair when we formalise our union at the kirk."

Cairstine smiled up at him. "I like it just as it is. Just you and me with Robbie to bear witness and no critical onlookers to please. Our own vows, ours and for us."

"My lady, I agree." Duncan pulled her close to his chest. "Nevertheless, we will still have to announce the banns and stand in front of the preacher for our marriage to be legal in England."

She kissed his neck. "I suppose so, but as far as I am concerned, we are a couple. However, I will be better able to bear the speculative glances and smirks without the urge to retort for knowing we are already wed and I am no trembling virgin."

"Will I no longer make you tremble after such a short time, sweetheart?"

She pressed against him. "You will set my skin aflame as you are now, forever, I have no doubt about that. Every inch of me tingles. I long for the touch of your fingers, your lips, your tongue and the hardness of your manhood thrusting between my legs."

His stiffening cock sprang to full attention at the desire he heard in her voice. He plucked on the bows of satin ribbon that fastened the back of her dress. "Sweet Jesu, my love. Get rid of this before you unman me too early with your words."

Cairstine stepped back with a small flirtatious smile that quirked the corners of her lips. She twitched the lacy wrap from her shoulders and held it between her hands. "Tut, tut, you are impatient, my lord. My garments must remain in good order tonight."

Oh so slowly, she folded her shawl and placed it over the back of a chair, then eased her dress down towards her waist. Duncan swallowed hard as her beautifully round breasts appeared, then harder at the sight of her russet muff as she allowed her dress to drop to the floor before she stepped out of it. His cock throbbed in time to the fast beat of his heart as he reached for her.

Cairstine took a step back and puckered him a kiss. "Ah, ah. Not yet."

His balls tightened as he watched her pick up her dress, soothe the creases from the skirt and drape it over her shawl. Then she turned towards him and met his gaze, the green of her irises darker and stormier than he'd ever seen them. "Now, I believe, it is you that is rather overdressed."

Duncan gazed at her nakedness and loosened his cravat. "You wedded me while not wearing so much as a petticoat beneath your gown? It is as well I didn't know."

She ran the tip of her tongue over her top lip and teased. "Perhaps I should invest in a pair of frilly underdrawers? I've heard they're becoming quite the thing for the younger, racier matrons of the beau monde."

"If the Lady Cairstine McColl was a hoyden, you, Countess of Callander, are a veritable hussy."

She smiled into his eyes. "Only for you, my husband. I promise it."

Duncan could wait no longer and stripped off his clothes with no thought given to the folding of anything at all. "And I you, my love." He scooped

Cairstine up, carried her to the bed and kissed her long, deep and hard as he lay over her. She kissed him back with a passion to match his own, with one hand exploring the hair on his chest while the other sought the tight curls at his groin.

He pinned her arms as his seed threatened to erupt from his cock before he had satisfied his lady, and she writhed beneath him when he moved his head and sucked on her pretty pink nipple. He meted the same treatment to the other and as she arched her back, ran his tongue down her torso and paused over her belly. She squirmed and squeaked. "Duncan? You can't kiss me *there.*"

He flicked his tongue into her central dimple and over her pubic mound, then tasted the sweet, juicy split between her legs. "Yes, I can, love."

She bucked. He released her arms, captured her hips and sucked, nibbled and investigated every sensitive crease until she begged. "Duncan, please…I need you."

"Then never let it be said I did not do as my lady needs." Duncan plunged his throbbing shaft inside her and she moaned.

"Oh, God."

He thrust deeper and harder. She raised her hips to meet his every stroke, her fingernails digging into his back, until she cried out her climax. "Oh, oh, oh…yesss."

Duncan thrust again and again and again then groaned when his final pleasure arrived. "My beautiful wife. I love you."

They stilled, breathing hard, and when his erection softened, Duncan rolled to his side and offered out his arm. Cairstine curled beneath it and sighed, her head resting on his chest. "Well, that was all I ever hoped for but with...um...ah...a little something I wasn't expecting?"

Duncan kissed into her hair, then breathed in deep and admitted, "I've had two mistresses who showed me the way to go on. Both experienced matrons, older than me." He felt Cairstine stiffen beside him. *Damn.* He cursed and could have hit himself. Not the right thing to say at that moment.

"And is either still in situ?"

"No, my love, nor will anyone ever be." *Pray God she believes me.* "Plus, I do not visit the fleshpots or the catteries in search of short-term relief. I never have and never will."

"Catteries?" Cairstine asked, then went crimson. "Ah yes, the worst brothels. I feel sorry for those poor women who have no option but to sell themselves there."

"As do most sensible men. I prefer the company of my hand to the risks to be found there."

She giggled. "Duncan!"

He laughed. "And if it pleases you, sweetheart, neither have I made love to its natural ending with anyone other than you. I did not wish to beget a child any more than the lady concerned wanted to conceive one, so I always withdrew and completed our final pleasure by other means."

She blushed as she nestled closer, stroked her fingers through his chest hair, then moved them towards his groin "I'm glad you haven't created a babe whose birth was desired by neither party. Would you like me to kiss you here, like you did me?"

His heart missed a beat and his mouth became dry. Duncan had to clear his throat before he could reply. "I would, oh so very much...but only if you would enjoy doing so. It has to be enjoyed by us both."

Cairstine tilted her head to one side, as if she were considering his statement. "I think I would like to try." She bit her lip. "No, I *know* I would like to try."

His cock had barely a twitch left in it for now, so he raised her searching hand to his lips and kissed it. "Mmm... We could kiss each other *there* at the same time later?"

She traced her fingertips around the outline of his lips. "Mmm...yes."

His stomach gave an unfortunate grumble and Cairstine giggled. "Oops. I think before that, you're in need of another serving of rabbit stew?"

Duncan smiled and admitted, "It was delicious, and we haven't eaten much these last two days."

Cairstine sat up and swung her legs off the bed. "True. I hope you'll still find it as good when we have it for supper and again for breakfast because there's no time to rustle up any alternative."

He watched her natural grace as she walked to the pot and inspected the contents, entirely comfortable in their mutual nakedness like no woman he'd ever known before. She dipped her finger in, raised it to her mouth and made a moue of distaste. "Urgh. It's far too cold. Get off the bed, lazybones, and rekindle the embers while I search in the packages."

Duncan grinned, did as ordered, and Cairstine passed him a coarse linen homespun shirt then covered herself with a clean but well-worn calico shift. She picked up his discarded clothes, smoothed them into a semblance of order then served the stew onto their plates. He spotted a corked flagon of ale, poured into two pottery mugs and set them on the table.

Cairstine added the platters of steaming stew and smiled. "Our wedding feast awaits."

They took their places. Duncan picked up his mug and toasted his bride. "And our first meal together as husband and wife. Stew and ale finer than any banquet, my love."

She smiled and sipped from her own mug, although her eyes were a little misty. "I would not change a thing other than I wish Papa could know of my happiness."

Duncan gripped her shoulder for a second. "He will know it in the end, sweetheart. What we undertake now is only for his sake. I will not see him suffer, but under the laws of the country we live in, we are wed. A lesser rank, I know, but you no longer bear your father's name. We will set out tomorrow and do everything we can to secure the letter, but should we fail, it will surely be of comfort to him that your future is assured?"

Cairstine lifted her chin, her eyes alive with the determination he knew and loved. "We will not fail. I will not allow it, no more than will you."

* * * *

The following morning they dressed in the homespun garments Robbie had left them and set off in the wagon for what Duncan called "*the beginning of their married life together*". It was slow going. A pair of highly bred carriage horses, or Duncan's curricle, could cover the distance in half the time, but the smaller beasts Robbie had supplied to suit their disguise for the next day or so could not move at such a pace and required frequent rest breaks.

"Robbie will be a lot faster and more comfortable than us," Cairstine remarked. "And no doubt enjoying the fact you trust him with your cattle."

"I trust him with my life—and yours, so why not my horses? He is as much of a brother to me as Fraser was, and has been more so since Fraser lost his life."

"True, and this mode of travel is quite enjoyably different. I've never sat high up on the box before."

* * * *

For the first couple of days Cairstine found the journey an adventure. They made love under the stars, washed in streams, ate what food they foraged and supplemented it with the supplies they had. All appeared to be going well.

With every mile they learnt a little more about each other. It was strange to think they had been friends all their lives but until then she hadn't known Duncan hated the local delicacy of hare in whisky. He loved hare and ditto whisky, just not together.

"I promise never to ask Cook to make you that," Cairstine said as they neared the border. "As long as you never make me eat oatmeal pudding. It's slimy, and yes, I know that is sacrilege. I prefer my oats in oatcakes."

Duncan laughed. "We must create a list." He looked up at the sky where the late afternoon sun was hazy. "We better make haste. I'm not liking this weather." Within seconds the mist descended—a typical Scottish summer mizzle.

The ghostly white mist took the heat from the sun and the dampness of it chilled Cairstine to the bone. Duncan halted the horses and retrieved two old, well-darned travelling cloaks from the wagon. She donned one of the garments and wished she could wear her own much thicker pelisse—currently folded in the bottom of her portmanteau—when the extra layer of clothing didn't mitigate her shivers, but the quality of it was too fine.

Duncan chaffed her hands, set the horses in motion at a fast near-trot and Cairstine was more than relieved when he pointed to a low, squat building up ahead. Not anything as grand as a staging post, but a country inn offering basic fare to working folk travelling the high road in pursuit of their employer's business.

He drove the wagon into the yard and unharnessed the horses to graze with others of their kind in a pasture at the back of the building.

Cairstine shivered and held her jaw tight. "Brr, my t…teeth are chattering, I am chilled beyond my bones."

Duncan took her hand and led her inside. "Come, love. Let's get you warm."

The opportunity to enter such a place had never come her way before and Cairstine looked around the inn's taproom with interest. It was busy with customers sat on benches at rough-hewn tables, but not overcrowded. A roaring fire heated the space and neat and tidy serving girls bustled about depositing bowls of what appeared to be mutton stew accompanied by a hunk of bread to those seated. The savoury aroma teased Cairstine's nostrils and her mouth watered. Duncan gestured towards a space at a table not too far from the fire and added their cloaks to those drying on a high-backed settle nearby.

Cairstine relaxed in the oh-so-welcome warmth. Duncan ordered a mug of watered beer for her, a jug of dark brew for himself and two portions of the only item on the menu, adding a touch of Robbie's lilting burr to his voice.

The food arrived. Cairstine tore lumps from the bread and used them, in the absence of a spoon, to scoop her stew into her mouth with an unladylike gusto that would have been deemed positively unseemly when dining in Polite Society.

Duncan grinned. "Fair clemmed are ye, love?"

"Aye."

The traveller sat to the side of Duncan smacked his lips then wiped them on the sleeve of his jacket. "Eeh…nowt amiss wi the scran 'ere, be there?"

It took Cairstine longer to decipher the unfamiliar northern English dialect than Duncan. He chuckled. "It's braw."

"Thas weather be reet misery. Yer best bide 'ere this night. I is, as are most. Innkeep said as he'd be happy for us ter bed down in t'warmth of the tap room till daybreak."

Duncan nodded his thanks for the information and their dining companion introduced himself.

"I be Will Farrow of York, travelling the road to deliver my master's postbag ter receiving office in Edinburgh."

Cairstine smiled as Duncan fibbed with great panache. "Dougan and my wife, Tina. We are making our way south to Newcastle, hoping for employment that pays more wages than we earn at home."

Will nodded sagely. "Newcastle, yer say? I just come from thataway. Road outta it be reet shocking. Yer nag could easy break a leg so broke up as it is. If yer'll heed a mite from me?"

Duncan nodded.

"Cross the border near Carter Bar but don't head for the Newcastle and coast, head fer the old drove road just afore Otterburn." He dipped his finger into his ale and drew a wet sketch on the table. "Here be the crossing. The drover's route branches orf here. He traced another damp line. "Travel a mile or so to the east then yer can drop down an' skirt Byrness—"

The man to Will's other side looked at the tabletop and interrupted. "Byrness? Thas a reet rough ol' track."

"Better'n t'other this time of year," Will stated mulishly.

"Mebbe...but I allus travels the main road." He looked at Duncan and offered his name. "John Dixon, carter, delivering 'ousehold goods to Edinburgh. What work yer seeking?"

Without suitable garb to provide the backstory of curate, Cairstine improvised. "Footman and lady's maid."

Will wiped the map away with his cuff. "Rumour is thas to be a great bridal thataway soon. Mebbe yer would do well to present yerselves at Armstrong House. More servants is bound to be needed wi a new bride about the place."

His companion drank deep from his tankard and shook his head, his face somber. "I would'ne work for the Armstrongs given the curse..."

Cairstine sat straighter. "Curse? What curse?"

John sat forwards and regarded her. "Well now... I were nowt but a nipper when ol' Granny Dixon died but she allus swore it were true being as she heard it from 'er own granny what was in service to the Armstrongs when she were young. Cursed they be an' by one of their own. Bad luck 'as followed 'em all ever since..."

Cairstine frowned. "Someone in the family wished ill-fortune on their own kin?" Duncan frowned at her and she realised she'd forgotten to disguise her voice. Luckily, neither John nor Will seemed to notice.

"Ye can tell they're nay Scotsmen," she added in a broader Scottish accent.

John took another draught of his ale and continued. "Great, Great Granny tellt as the daughter of the 'ouse, Sarah Armstrong, were to wed a grand lord until 'e caught sight of another and jilted 'er at the altar. The lass were beside 'erself and harangued 'er family afterwards for arranging a union that left 'er a spinster…for who else would want ta marry a woman what 'ad been rejected like that? The family found a husband for 'er in t'end but 'e was allus second best an' she did nowt but let 'im know it. Granny said Sarah got more bitter an' full o' spite each passing year and wi'er dying breath cursed the Armstrongs to never prosper until a McColl woman, like 'ad caused her misery, endured a wretched marriage like she 'ad… Them Armstrongs are a bad 'uns, and the old man? He be worst o'lot."

Cairstine dug her fingernails into Duncan's thigh.

He covered her hand with his, gave it a reassuring squeeze then yawned. "Thenk ye for warning us. It's fair awfy tae see thon unhappiness in a family. Ah guess it falls on those who serve them, an' aw, eh? We'll steer muckle clear o' they Armstrongs."

Duncan stood and tugged Cairstine to her feet. "Come awa', wife. Enough o' the blether. We've travelled yon far the day and there's a fair few more miles to gan the morra. Thank ye, sir, fae the craic."

Cairstine choked down the instinctive retort that rose to her lips at his bossy manner, pasted a doe-like look of compliance onto her face and followed his lead. "Aye, husband. Of course. As ere, ye are richt."

Duncan's eyes glinted his appreciation of her play-acting as he retrieved their now warm and dry cloaks. An empty corner of the room beckoned and, wrapped in their outer garments, they lay down on the hard but clean-swept floor.

Cairstine resisted the urge to snuggle closer to Duncan, given the onlookers in the room, and maintained a respectable distance as she whispered, "That can't be the hidden reason behind all this, can it? Surely no man of sense could believe in the power of curses in this enlightened age?"

Duncan snorted. "I'd like to know how much spirit he imbibes."

"You think he's maybe a sot?"

He chuckled. "If he's thinking that way, I'm suspecting half a bottle of brandy with breakfast at the very least, my love."

Cairstine giggled then yawned as the long day caught up with her and, heedless of any other in the room, curled into Duncan's side as her eyelids fluttered closed.

# Chapter Seven

Duncan gazed at his sleeping wife then pulled her into arms so her head was cushioned on his chest rather than the floor.

*Fully dressed, the rest of the room can go to hell in a handcart.*

Cairstine nestled closer and emitted a sleepy sigh through lips he longed to kiss. Around them the room quietened as weary travellers found their own spots of floor space or stretched out on the benches. Duncan relaxed and considered John's words—for in every tall tale there was a grain of truth.

Bad luck and failing fortunes could be blamed on a curse, he supposed, if a man's brain was addled through drink or worse. But what then if a certain letter had opportunely fallen into that man's hands? The thing was...which man?

If was the senior, a man of Cairstine's papa's age, the reasoning behind the attempt to blackmail him into insisting she marry an Armstrong made sense—even if the thinking behind the scheme was scrambled. The fact that the letter *existed* was the point. It had the power to cause irretrievable harm to the McColls and as such must be found and destroyed.

He fell asleep with a wry smile upon his lips—as troublesome as the letter was, it had gifted him his beautiful bride, so he couldn't feel it was totally abhorrent. Just the opposite.

* * * *

Cairstine stirred first in the morning and nudged him awake. She smiled up at him. "I cannot believe we have spent the night cuddling like this in a less-than-private room." She looked around at those still sleeping, those stretching and those getting ready to leave. "Although, seeing so many people, I think we were lucky to even find some floor to pass the night on, scandalous or not."

Duncan kissed her nose. "We are married—in the eyes of all Scotland anyway, and at least the patronesses of Almack's are not present."

Cairstine giggled. "That is just as well. Could you imagine that scene? Or maybe I could say, I wish they were. Then they would never trouble me again."

Duncan squeezed his arm around her. "They have no hold over you now. We shall do your come out for Scotland in Edinburgh and your first proper season London if you wish, but you are a married lady and safe from their disapproval."

She stroked his cheek. "And very happy to be so."

He patted her rear. "Up with you before I scandalize the place and kiss you."

Cairstine stretched and stood. "Is there a private chanty, do you suppose?"

The buxom farmer's wife lying on the settle a little way behind them answered. "A chanty? You mean a privy?"

Cairstine nodded.

"They do, dearie, but only for us females. The men 'as ter use the greenery on offer outside. Come wiv me."

Duncan grinned and Cairstine followed the woman to earth closet. He bought half a loaf of bread at the kitchen door, walked outside and put it in the wagon before he found a convenient bush to pee in. He was harnessing the horses when Cairstine pushed open the door to the chanty. She glanced down at her hands when she reached him. "I feel so grubby having slept in my day clothes. There was not so much as a jug of cold water to wash in or wipe my hands after…." She gestured towards the outhouse.

Duncan reached down, plucked at a clump of wet, dewy grass and handed it to her. "We should reach West Woodburn today. Strange how we were told to go that way by Will. I checked and it's not that much longer to Newcastle—if we were indeed going there. A good cover for us. Rub this between your palms, love. It's the best I can do for now."

She did while he finished harnessing the horses then they sat side by side on the bench seat of the wagon and he set the horses to trot.

The sun rose higher and warmed them with no sign of the previous day's bad weather. The views were wide as the hills rolled away into the distance with the farthest ones a misty blue. Somewhere nearby a curlew called and was answered. The horses startled a grouse, which squawked and flew up into the air with a whirring of wings. Duncan stopped the cart.

"What is it?" Cairstine asked, alarm in her tone. "Who is it? Where?"

"A moment." Duncan held the horses steady while he scanned the area.

Nothing else stirred. "Just the horses giving a grouse a surprise."

There was no one in sight, much to his relief. The last thing they wanted to do was draw notice to themselves. Cairstine sighed. "Thank the Lord. How much farther?"

"Maybe too far for today. However better slow and steady than not at all. The nags are sturdy, but even so, we are asking a lot from them."

"True enough. Slow and steady it will be. At least it gives us time to refine our plans." Cairstine settled back down beside him as they moved on.

After two hours Duncan called a halt and released the horses to graze. "We have time to stop, rest the horses and eat. Let me see if there is anything edible around here."

Cairstine brewed a pan of nettle tea on the campfire he had built them and set it aside to cool and take on more flavour. She used their other pan to cook the wild mushrooms he'd foraged while she was collecting more wood and ladled their meaty goodness onto slices of bread.

"I'd hate to have to cope with so little forever," she remarked as she washed their few utensils in a tiny burn. No more than a trickle, it wasn't easy to dunk anything deep enough to clean effectively, but she did her best. "It's a novelty for now, and I'm pleased to be able to cope, but the thought of always living like this..." She shuddered as she again used grass to dry things. "I will be ever grateful we don't have to."

"No wanderer then?" Duncan put the fire out and made sure no spark or warmth remained before he wiped his hands on the grass. "You prefer some comforts? I confess, so do I. I had enough of rough living before, when working for the Crown." He gestured towards a convenient bush. "If you need to go..."

Cairstine smiled. "I think I'd better."

Humans and beasts refreshed, Duncan set the wagon in motion again. "I want to get as far as we can before that nasty cloud over yonder arrives here. It could spell bad weather."

"Then by all means let's move on quickly. I do not fancy a soaking."

They didn't stop again until they'd bumped their way over the forest track though the Kielder Forest after they'd skirted Byrness. They rejoined the main road and he smiled. "Not far now and we will arrive at the Grey Horse. I should have told Robbie to drive my curricle up the road each day to intercept us. It will cause less comment if we present ourselves at the staging post in the guise we will be using going forwards."

Whether it was the power of wishful thinking or not, Duncan was delighted when he caught sight of his curricle on the side of the road. He halted behind it and jumped down from the bench seat. "I am glad to see you."

Robbie's eyes twinkled. "I thought mebbe ye might be, if ye are quite sure you've had enough of a honeymoon?"

Cairstine giggled as Duncan objected, "Honeymoon be damned. We shall have a proper one after we visit the kirk."

Robbie chuckled, hefted their portmanteaus from the wagon and secured them on the curricle. Cairstine glanced at her homespun dress. "That we should arrive in your curricle is one thing but what about our clothes? I have my pelisse with me. I can hide beneath it until I can bathe and change into suitable attire but you…?"

"Nay, dinnae fret, my lady. His lordship's caped driving coat is in his," Robbie said. "I did ma best tae get all needed."

"Robbie, you think of everything."

He blushed. "Dinnae gan on, m'lady. Like ah said, I jest dae ma best."

"Your best is superb." Cairstine kissed his cheek, which made him blush even more. Mindful of his embarrassment, she then left him alone. She and Duncan covered their tatty outfits with their rather more superior cloaks, and with a few instructions from Duncan to his friend, they left Robbie to follow on behind them in the wagon. The prime bloodstock ate up the miles and in no time they halted in the inn's yard. Duncan gave the reins to an ostler and muttered after he assisted her dismount, "Let the acting commence. I am the neighbour obliging your father. You are the pea goose that's boring me to death."

Cairstine curtsied. "As you wish, my lord."

Duncan grinned, led her into the inn then looked down the length of his aristocratic nose and spoke in tones that dared anyone to question why the female of quality at his side was unchaperoned. "Two rooms and a chambermaid to attend the lady, if you please. Her servant is indisposed."

The Grey Horse might not have been one of the major staging posts on the route between Scotland and England, but it was well set up. The proprietor didn't hesitate to bow and assure them of immediate and excellent service. "Of course, my lord. At once." He clicked his fingers and the bell boy sprang to attention. "Rooms twenty and twenty-one…"

Duncan huffed. "No, my good man. Not adjoining in the absence of my companion's lady's maid. Whatever can you be thinking of?"

The owner's cheeks reddened at his mistake. "Yes…yes… My apologies, but they are the best I have on offer. Perhaps room twenty for the lady and room fifteen for your lordship, if you don't mind it being at the back of the house?"

Duncan nodded his assent and drawled, "Very well. We shall require a private parlour for supper—"

Cairstine chirped up in missish tones that, accompanied by coyly lowered eyelids, nearly caused Duncan to choke. "With the door set ajar to observe the proprieties, I thank you…"

The proprietor bowed his acknowledgement and they followed the young lad up the stairs. He opened the door to a large and sunny room. "Room twenty, Miss. I'll fetch yer luggage an' Bessie will be wi yer short as."

Duncan looked at her over his head. "We shall dine at seven. Do not be late."

Cairstine tossed her curls. "You would prefer to starve me, I'm sure. So, if I must, yes." She stepped inside the room and shut the door with a sharp snap behind her.

Duncan maintained an expression of bland indifference as he was shown to his room, which was half the size of Cairstine's and gloomily darker. He forbore to comment but ordered a pail of hot water to be delivered along with his luggage, and chuckled at his wife's acting skills after the servant left. His portmanteau arrived within fifteen minutes, but it was a full hour later before his washing water appeared. The boy staggered in with it. "Beggin' yer pardon, it's not over 'ot, but yer lady ordered a bath to 'er room an' it took all the 'ot water we 'ad in the kitchen to fill it."

Duncan dismissed the lad with a sixpence for his trouble then stripped and began to sluice down. He washed his chest, arms and shoulders then moved the soapy washcloth down towards his groin. His cock hardened as he imagined slipping into the same bath as Cairstine and exploring the soft creases between her legs with his soapy fingers—until a door slamming in the distance recalled him. He doused his unruly shaft with cold water from the jug standing to one side of the washstand and dressed using his own prowess to arrange his cravat. His jacket fitted as tightly as it should across his shoulders when he shrugged it on and he carefully disarranged his hair and stepped out the room, as near 'a la mode' perfection as would suffice outside of the capital.

He tapped on the door of Cairstine's room. The chambermaid opened it and bobbed. The scent of violets tickled his senses. He looked past her, saw Cairstine clothed as she had been on their wedding day, but with her red curls dressed high on her head, accentuating the delicate beauty of her face.

*My love, my wife…mine*

He swallowed hard, remembered his part and offered out his arm with a show of reluctance as he drawled, "Come along."

Cairstine sighed then announced in tragic tones worthy of Sarah Siddons as she laid her hand upon it, "I shall not be able to swallow so much as a morsel, but I will make the attempt rather than waste away as *some* people might prefer." She smirked up at him as he led her down the stairs, a spark of devilment lighting her eye, then proceeded to eat her dinner accompanied by dramatic utterances intended to be heard by anyone lurking on the other side of the half-closed door. "Oh, I couldn't possibly...beef sirloin cooked in red wine is much too rich for my taste. No, my lord, do not place buttered asparagus on my plate. It does not sit well with me and will plague me all night as will the kidneys coddled with cream and mustard..."

Duncan snorted as she tucked into each of the dishes on offer with relish then grinned his appreciation when she wiped her bread around her plate and left not a sign that she had eaten anything at all. Her mournful look at the servant that came into the room to remove the plates from the table nearly undid him completely and he walked her back up to her room, fighting the urge to give her pert bottom a soft pinch for being such a teasing minx.

Bessie, the chambermaid, waited inside the bedchamber when Cairstine opened the door, so he wished her a bored 'goodnight' and walked away. His own room did not look any more inviting than it had before supper, and even though the bed contained a feather-filled mattress he would gladly have swapped it for another night on a clean-swept floor with Cairstine's head resting on his chest.

He heard other doors opening and closing as he loosened his cravat and a still quietness seemed to settle over the place as he undressed. The bedsheets looked thankfully clean when he pulled the coverlet, but as he closed the bed curtains the latch on his door rattled…

* * * *

Cairstine undressed quickly and slid under the covers with a peevish, "This bed is as comfortable as a thorn bush. What on earth is the mattress made of?" It pained her to appear such a monster, but if she had to act a petulant person, she couldn't afford to let the façade slip.

The chambermaid blushed. "'Tis the best we have, m'lady. New last Michaelmas, it was."

Cairstine nodded. "Then I best make the most of it." She wriggled until she was comfortable and smiled at the chambermaid. It was so unfair to take her apparent annoyance out on the girl. "It's not your fault. Now I'll try and sleep as no doubt we will be off at some silly hour."

The maid curtseyed and left the room quietly. When she shut the door behind her, Cairstine sat up again and hugged her knees over the covers. It was time to plot.

Slowly the sounds of the inn and its occupants died down, until she heard a nearby clock sound twelve. Then the only noises were the rustle of the trees and the hooting of an owl. The floor outside her room creaked and she heard the low voice of the innkeeper say something, to be answered by someone else, whom she presumed was his wife.

Then once more all was silent. Cairstine waited until the clock chimed the half-hour then slid carefully out of bed. Her toes curled as they hit the wooden floor and she thrust them hastily in her slippers, which the maid had thoughtfully placed beside the bed. Now to find her pelisse. That was hung on the back of the door. She donned it, gathered it closely around her and opened her door, pleased it didn't squeak as she closed it behind her.

Luckily, she'd noted where room fifteen was, and that it was in the direction of the main stairs. If anyone came across her, she could always say she'd left her reticule downstairs or some such thing. The fact she should have rung for a maid to go and look for it could be a complication, but she decided she'd face that if it happened.

Creaky floorboards could also cause problems. In fact, the whole twenty or so yards were full of pitfalls. However, the trip had to be done. Resolute, she trod carefully along the corridor, thankful there was enough moonlight to add a glow to the infrequent candles flickering in their sconces.

*I should be glad they are still lit.* It seemed the inn left them alight for their patrons until the wicks were finished.

The hall outside room fifteen was almost in full darkness, the nearest sconce empty. Cairstine checked no one was around—though what difference it would make, for she was the one skulking in the corridor, she had no idea—and lifted the latch. A sudden thought struck her. What if he'd locked the door? After all it was a public inn, and not all patrons could be assumed to be good, honest, God-fearing citizens.

To her relief, he hadn't. Probably, she reasoned, so the servant could come in with his shaving water or whatever. She slid through the tiniest aperture possible and closed the door quietly behind her as she took stock of her bearings. Ahead, the bed, nowhere as big as the one she'd just left—was half hidden behind curtains.

The window shutters were open, but little light entered the room. Perhaps a good idea for some, but as husband and wife she concluded it wasn't relevant in their situation.

If they dare acknowledge it.

"Who's there?" Duncan's voice was alert, not at all sleep-filled. "Reveal yourself."

The curtain around the bed swung open and he stood up, as naked as the day he was born. There was enough light for Cairstine to see that. Her mouth went dry and she swallowed heavily. "It's me. I thought we could use some time to talk without risk of being overheard."

Duncan lit the taper and unselfconsciously pulled his banyan on. "Then in the interests of being able to talk coherently," he said with a wry smile, "maybe do not reveal yourself."

Cairstine laughed. "Perhaps not, though, your, er, reveal, was rather nice."

Duncan waggled his finger at her. "What have I unleashed?" he teased as he stirred the embers into a glow and added a few more logs to get the fire blazing once more. He patted the sole chair in the room. "Come and sit with me. It at least has a padded seat, if little else to recommend it.'

"You have unleashed your wife," Cairstine said as she sat on Duncan's lap. Really, the man was incorrigible. She wriggled to get comfortable and he groaned.

"Love, if you do that we will get no talking done at all…" He held her in place and kissed the top of her head. "So, before my mind becomes clouded with thoughts of a carnal nature. Thoughts I would have no trouble in translating into actions."

A rush of heat suffused Cairstine. She could tell fine-well how easily his thoughts could become actions. Indeed, a certain part of his anatomy was making its presence felt as it nestled against her rear. "I see what you mean," she said shakily. "I will stay as still as Lot's wife."

He laughed. "No need to go quite that far." He grasped her waist and settled her buttocks onto his thigh rather than his crotch. "So, to recap our current situation. We no longer need the wagon as we can now resume our natural positions in the ton. In the morning I'll ask Robbie to arrange for the wagon and the nags to be boarded with a local farmer. He can then assume the role of tiger and travel with us on the backboard of the curricle."

Cairstine nodded. "I agree. Even if he is a little overgrown in both size and years, it will still add to our appearance of respectability if we arrive at Armstrong's house accompanied by a servant rather than my being completely unchaperoned."

"True. Then we—"

Duncan was interrupted by the sound of hoofbeats outside followed by a loud shout of, "Hoy there, Ostler."

"Someone is in a hurry," Cairstine commented, sitting straighter to peer through the window to see what the commotion was all about.

Duncan held her still on his lap as she started to rise. "No, don't look out. This is not your room, remember. Let me."

She tilted her body sideways to allow him to stand and wrinkled her nose. Of course, it made sense, but she was as nosy as the next person. "Tell me then."

He parted the curtains, opened the sash a few inches and peered out, then whistled softly. "Well, well."

"Well, well what?" Cairstine did her best to curb her impatience. "What can you see? Can you hear anything?"

"A man, demanding a horse as his has lost a shoe. Saying he has to go north in a hurry. And the landlord calling him Mr Armstrong." He drew back from the window. "I might just have to dress and return downstairs to demand brandy as I cannot sleep." He grinned, his teeth white in the dark room. "Perhaps you should stop here until I come back?"

Cairstine nodded. She was happy to do so. "You may be certain of it, for I will be eaten up with curiosity."

Duncan swiftly donned breeches, shirt and boots, shrugged into a jacket and bent to kiss his lady on the lips. "I will not be long. Stir the fire up if need be." He left the room quietly.

Cairstine stared at the fire. If wait she must, she intended to be comfortable, so she removed herself to the bed and pulled the coverlet around her. That was better.

# Chapter Eight

Duncan took the stairs two at a time and paused on the half landing. To be seen or not? Either option had strengths and weaknesses. The decision was taken from him as the door at the top of the stairs opened and a short, stout gentleman clad in a frogged dressing gown and embroidered slippers stepped out.

"What's amiss?" he barked, in a tetchy way. "Why have I been awoken from my sleep? Are those marauding Scots of old on the move? Border Reivers or just damned noisy buggers?"

"I have no idea." Duncan tempered his accent in favour of more polished tones. "That's what I was about to try and discover."

"Ha, wait a second, I'm coming with you." The man shut his bedchamber door. "Joshua Ferris from North Shields at your service. Shoes and leather goods. Did a diversion north to see a promising newcomer."

Duncan bowed. "Sir David Livermore of Leicestershire. On business, but also accompanying my ward south. The commotion woke me as well."

They reached the front hall as an ostler, two servants and a many-caped gentleman bustled in from the stable yard.

The landlord appeared from a back room, looking visibly upset. "Gentlemen, what can I do for you?"

The newcomer and Joshua Ferris both opened their mouths at once. Duncan stood by patiently, wondering who would get the first words in.

The landlord ignored both men and turned to Duncan. "Sir?"

Duncan smiled. "I've just come to see what the commotion is all about and enquire whether I may be of any assistance to a fellow traveller?"

The newcomer took a step forwards. "Not unless you are a blacksmith or have a horse I can borrow or buy. It is imperative I ride north, now and at great speed."

"Sadly, neither," Duncan told him before turning to the landlord. "Perhaps our host can oblige you?"

The landlord frowned distractedly. "Well… Yes… And no… What I mean is I don't have a mount I can spare, but I can send a boy to rouse the village blacksmith. I can't see the shoeing being accomplished with any great speed though. Blackie will have banked and damped the fire for the night. It will have to be stoked and brought up to temperature."

Mr Ferris seemed as keen as Duncan to discover what the new arrival's business could be. "Well, as we're all now wide awake, I suggest we take a glass of port in my parlour?"

Their late-night guest huffed his impatience at the landlord for the delay. "Don't dally, then. Send the boy at once. Get the work underway." Then he recovered his good manners and acquiesced to the invitation with a small bow towards Mr Ferris. "An hour in a warm parlour accompanied by a glass will be most welcome, I thank you."

Duncan permitted himself a wry smile as he turned to follow the two men. Cairstine would be in a fever of impatience he was sure but the chance of discovering whether this was indeed George Armstrong – and even perhaps why he was heading north when they were travelling in the opposite direction, supposedly to meet him – was just too good to miss. The parlour fire was reanimated by way of the poker and a fresh shovelful of coal from the scuttle, Duncan settled back into the depths of his over-stuffed chair. The landlord offered a tray. He accepted a glass then turned it so the deep ruby liquid glowed in the lamp light. *Hmm... Not too shabby for an inn.*

The inn's reluctant guest was the first to speak. "I can't believe my bloody horse cast a shoe. My own farrier visited only last week. I'll be having words with him when I return home to Corbridge."

*So, it could be him.*

Mr Ferris sipped and enquired, "Your business seems to be of some urgency, sir?"

His guest raised his glass and made his name known, as was only polite, having accepted Ferris' hospitality. "George Armstrong, pleased to make your acquaintance."

*Yes.* Duncan smiled his satisfaction and fibbed as he responded in kind. "Sir David Livermore, travelling south with my ward."

"Timothy Ferris. It is an honour to meet you both, even under these odd circumstances."

To Duncan's further satisfaction, like a dog with a bone, Ferris did not let his original question go and asked again, "And your urgency is…?"

"I need to get to Scotland post-haste, and not by the mail. I have to avert a calamity…plus, I need to get back within the week." He rested his chin on his cravat and sighed deeply. "Families, why do we put up with them?"

Duncan probed a little deeper with another untruth and added a fake sigh to match Armstrong's own. "You have my sympathy, sir. We should not speak ill of our nearest relatives, I know, but my father at times is enough to drive me to distraction."

Ferris sipped and nodded sagely.

Armstrong leant forwards and tapped his finger on one side of his nose. "We're all men of the world here, so I'll admit my father has come up with the most cockamamie scheme."

Duncan held his breath. "He has…?

Armstrong blinked then shook his head as if he'd realised he was on the point of saying too much and swallowed the remainder of his port. "It's only a bit of nonsense he's got hold of." He stood. "But you must excuse me, gentlemen. I will accomplish nothing further tonight if I take more than one glass, so I'll bid you good evening and make my way to the smithy." He left the room.

"My cue as well," Duncan said. "Or I will be fit for naught tomorrow."

Ferris struggled out of the over-stuffed armchair he had chosen to settle in. "Nor me."

Duncan opened the door courteously and they made their way upstairs.

Now to tell Cairstine what he'd learnt—possibly after he'd soothed her fiery temper. She must be seething by now. He let himself into his bedroom and waited for the explosion, which didn't come.

She was asleep.

*It has been an exhausting day. Should I wake her, or let her get what sleep she can?*

Duncan considered for a moment, found a tablet of paper and a pencil, scribbled a few words, then lifted Cairstine and carried her to her own room. She stirred only briefly as he laid her down. The note he propped where she would see it as soon as she woke, on the small table beside her bed. That done, he headed back to his own room to snatch a few hours' rest.

* * * *

Cairstine woke with a start at the jangle of curtains being moved and blinked to clear the sleepy fog from her mind. She was back in her own room. How? She had no memory of returning there. She opened one eye to see the fresh-faced maid of the night before indicate a bowl of water and a fresh, clean towel.

"There's yer water, Miss. It's still warm and the genlmum says half an hour for breakfast in the parlour. I tried to tell 'im it were a bit on the tight side, but 'e were 'aving none of it. Do you need me to 'elp yer?"

Cairstine unscrambled her brain to understand the maid's words. "Ah, no, thank you. I can cope. If you could let my guardian know I'll be there, please?"

The maid curtseyed and left the room. Cairstine sat up and spied the folded paper on the table beside her bed. She opened it and read…

*Good morning, my love. Forgive me for not waking you when I returned to my room last night. You looked so peaceful I couldn't bring myself to do so and carried you back to your own. I do have important news that will alter our plans though, so hurry to our private parlour as soon as you can? I'm intending to be up before times, so will hopefully have set the ball rolling in advance of our eating breakfast.*

*D*

Happy to have had the matter explained, Cairstine threw back the covers and, eager to hear Duncan's news hurried out of bed, had the shortest wash on record and scrambled into her travelling clothes. The hooks and buttons might not be the easiest things to do up alone, but there was no way she could let the maid see the tell-tale marks of love on her body from the passionate nights they had spent under the stars together prior to their arriving at the inn.

Her gaze lingered on the red marks on her breasts and upper legs before she hid them with her chemise and gown. The red mark on her neck was less easily covered. A lover's bite, Duncan had called it as he'd traced it with one long finger. A deep sucking motion, to draw the skin into one's mouth, followed by an arousing nip over the same place.

He'd seemed to enjoy the reciprocal one she had given him on his neck. Which of course, he could cover with a cravat, but she would have to improvise. Cairstine glanced at the clock and yelped—time was running out. She rummaged in her portmanteau and pulled out a lacy fichu and with that artfully draped around her neck she once more appeared the demure young lady she had to portray.

The landlord was just carrying a loaded tray into their private room as she rounded the corner from the stairwell.

"Perfect timing."

Duncan looked at her, his voice bland, but his expression—unseen by the landlord, who was busy putting the contents of the tray onto the table—was all she could hope for.

Loving, hot, arousing, and with the promise of more delights to come.

She curtseyed, agog to hear what he had to relay, but, she hoped, without the least sign of that being so on her face. "As you dictated, here I am."

The landlord gave each of them a wary glance and departed in a hurry.

Cairstine handed Duncan a slice of warm bread. "Poor man, I'm sure he expects an unseemly brawl or commotion from our play-acting. I think he'll be glad we're moving on today."

Duncan winked. "No doubt... But keep to your role as we speak lest any flapping ears overhear us?"

Cairstine wiped hedgerow jam from her face and fingers and squeaked. "My lord, do not think to tempt me with jam and honey..."

Duncan leant closer and lowered his voice. "Our late-night guest was definitely 'our' George Armstrong and he's heading north, although he wouldn't tell me why. From what he did say, he's not expecting you to arrive in Corbridge until next week and yes, this plot is not of his devising, but his father's. His words did not lead me to think he's an agreeable partner in the blackmail, but still, he could be hurrying north to put pressure on your father, so until we know differently I think we should presume he is."

Cairstine's eyes widened. He nudged his knee with hers. She understood his message and picked up her breakfast cup. "Hot chocolate with cream? How dare you!"

He smiled his appreciation and continued. "As Armstrong is not at home to receive you, I think we should rent a house in Corbridge. It will give us the freedom to come and go without undue comment or curiosity while we discover what we can about the Armstrong household, and possibly inveigle ourselves with some of his acquaintances. With that in mind, I've sent Robbie to speed on ahead in the curricle to arrange matters. For ourselves, a hired carriage awaits us outside."

It sounded good but, as ever, Cairstine's mind raced as she thought of possible pitfalls. "When locals call on us will they not wonder at my lack of a chaperone?" she asked. "That is one thing that is bothering me. I'm sure I will think of others." She smiled to show she realised how annoying that trait could be.

"Good point," Duncan conceded. "The house will be rented fully staffed, so a senior housemaid can suffice for a day or two while I visit agencies and hire a respectable widow to fulfil the role."

Cairstine harrumphed under her breath. "That sounds unpleasant. Would one be agreeable to come for such a short period of time?"

He nodded. "There will be a candidate or two for the position, I am certain. I envisage an older lady who requires a little additional income to top up her mite and wouldn't welcome any fuller commitment."

She wrinkled her nose. "Still, Armstrong being from home delays our searching his house for the letter. We will not receive an invitation to visit until he returns, and I had hoped to have the matter resolved sooner rather than later."

Duncan squeezed her hand. "Don't be disheartened, my love. We will call to leave our cards and pray we find Armstrong Senior in residence even though his son is not. I have a feeling he may be easier to persuade to part with the information we require."

Cairstine thought of the possibilities. "Yes. If he's already addled, he very well might tell us what we need to know. If only we can find that blasted letter."

"*When* we find it," Duncan said firmly. "Shall we depart?"

The door creaked and Cairstine resumed her part with a bored sigh. "I suppose so. If we must."

She got to her feet as the landlord re-entered the room.

A close shave from being overheard. She must remember the old adage, *walls may have ears.*

"Anything else, sir?"

"No, that was ample. If you would prepare my bill please, and arrange for our belongings to be brought down? We must be off."

"Going far?" the landlord asked, relief in his voice. No doubt at the thought of them departing without any disturbing scenes.

"To Leicester." Duncan's voice faded as Cairstine headed for the door.

*I must remember Leicester.*

There was no need as less than half an hour later they were on the way south, with little more interaction from the landlord except for a perfunctory farewell.

"Did you not tip him enough?" Cairstine asked. "He appeared rather grumpy."

"Ha. Not me. It seems Ferris, whom I met last night, did not tip at all. He informed the landlord, within my hearing, that the bed was lumpy, the wine inferior and the chicken a tough, aged hen. The landlord was not happy."

"Oh dear, I bet he wasn't. I can't say I agree, can you?" Cairstine settled herself more comfortably against the carriage squabs.

Duncan shook his head. "For the modest inn it is, I think the service was over and above what one should have expected. I tipped as handsomely as one befitting my supposed status would be able."

Cairstine nodded, leant against him and closed her eyes. Nights spent on hard ground and lumpy straw pallets had not proved restful and the lack of sleep was catching up with her. To say nothing of her newly discovered aches and pains. Those though, she would suffer again with pleasure to discover the arousal she achieved while gaining then.

*Many more times, I hope.*

She closed her eyes and dozed as the gentle sway of the carriage lured her into a semi-somnambulant state.

* * * *

Duncan gazed at the russet hair of his love as she slumbered, resting in his arms. No wonder she couldn't stay awake. He himself wouldn't have found it easy except with Cairstine so close his body was tight, his cock rigid and every sense on high alert.

He smiled to herself as she snuggled closer to him, and he swore she mumbled something like 's'lovely, my love' and smiled in her sleep. He had to agree. If only he could take things further. Wake her with a caress of her breasts, lift her skirts and tease her muff and...

*Enough. This is neither the time nor the place.*

He sighed and wriggled into a more comfortable position as he pondered his morning's work so far. He been up and busy a good two hours before he'd asked for Cairstine to be woken up. He'd written a letter for Robbie to present to a Corbridge solicitor to facilitate the rental of a house, along with the provision of a cook-cum-housekeeper, a butler, a groom and two housemaids. It was the least number of people they could cope with to run the house and he'd offered the excuse of requiring only a short-term lease for not engaging a full complement of staff.

Sadly, the presence of live-in servants would put paid to any intimacy between him and Cairstine—although that in itself provided an extra incentive to bring their business to an early resolution so far as he was concerned. He pictured them attending the local kirk to regularize their union as soon as they returned home, making any future subterfuge unnecessary—and from there it was only a short step to imagining bouncing upon his knee the red-haired child they would have. Or several. Perhaps three boys and two girls...

He grinned at that particular flight of fancy. It would be his fiery wife who decided how many children she would bear, and she would surely box his ears for presuming otherwise. The coach began to descend a steep hill. A stone marker on the roadside showed they were nearing Corbridge, so he gently shook Cairstine awake.

She blinked and yawned. "Oh, lud, did I fall asleep? Grief, I hope I didn't snore."

"No, just made some lovely snuffling noises." He laughed as she punched him lightly on the shoulder.

"How horrid. You make me sound like a pig."

"Not at all, my love, it was sweet."

Cairstine wrinkled her nose. "I'm not sure that is any better to be honest." She looked out of the window. "Where are we?"

"Not far from our destination. I asked the landlord this morning and there is a post house on the main road into Corbridge. Robbie will meet us there, hopefully accompanied by a solicitor bearing the keys to our house rental."

She nodded. "It's been fun," she said slowly. "I wouldn't want to have it as my lifestyle so that is one thing I have learnt from it all. But to be unknown was good. So was, ah…our exercise." She winked and Duncan guffawed.

"Very true."

"Now it's time for us to be a lord and a lady again, I suppose?"

Duncan nodded. "It is, my love. If Sir Richard and his unknown ward call at Armstrong house, they may or may not be received. The Earl of Callander and Lady McColl, however, will be whisked straight through to the drawing room. Knowing George is travelling north, we have a little leeway to discover what we can without having to deal directly with Armstrong's prospective marriage plans. In fact, I'm betting Armstrong Senior will put himself out to be welcoming and entertain us at his house."

"In case I hate the place and bolt? Which I do, and would, but won't."

He put his arms around her and held her close to his chest. "We will do everything in our power to protect your father and the honour of the McColl name. But if the worse comes to worse, you are my wife and a Callander now—and should the English court, be it ever so high, attempt to declare our wedding vows invalid for not having made in a church, they can go to hell. I will never repudiate our marriage as the Prince of Wales did to Maria Fitzherbert. I love you."

Cairstine smiled up at him. "I know it and love you too."

The coach slowed and a substantial inn came into view. They pulled into its yard, busy with ostlers and maids running to and fro. Duncan exchanged a grin with Cairstine at the sight of his curricle with Robbie sat on the box.

He handed her from the coach. Robbie jumped down from the box, handed the reins to an ostler and joined them. "I did as you said, my lord. Looked at the quality of the gold lettering on the law office windows and picked one of pristine appearance. Atterlee and Sons. Mr Atterlee awaits you inside. A portly gentleman wearing the pinstriped trews and waistcoat of his calling."

Duncan thanked Robbie and Cairstine looked enquiringly at him, so he explained. "Appearances aren't everything, but it has been my experience that businesses who spend coin to maintain their premises are able to do so because they are more successful in their field than their shabbier counterparts."

She nodded, then a small frown creased her brow. "While we're talking of appearances, I'd best wait inside the coach while you discuss matters with Mr

Atterlee. If I close the window blind, you can lead him to believe there's a chaperone with me."

The thought of his wife having to hide rather than being able to walk inside alongside him with a wedding band on proud display irked him. "Let's get about our business then. The sooner we find that damn letter and put an end to this, the better."

# Chapter Nine

Cairstine climbed back into the coach with a smile at her husband's impatience. She rather suspected Armstrong Senior and his son would be torn limb from limb if they didn't yield the letter. Still, she acknowledged, it would be preferable to discover where it was hidden without putting him to the trouble of having to expend the effort.

Duncan did not keep her waiting very long and joined her inside the coach, a rough-drawn map in his hand, not half an hour later. He grinned. "Mr Atterlee sends his regards along with his hopes for your swift recovery, my love."

"From what?"

His grin widened. "The motion of the coach leaves my ward rather green around the gills. He was more than relieved to hand over the keys rather than being obliged to accompany us to the house, especially after I hinted at the sour odour currently surrounding you."

The picture that conjured up.

*Horrible man.*

Cairstine punched his shoulder "Duncan! You wretch. Have you told him I am covered in vomit?"

He laughed and held his hands up in mock surrender. "No. No. Only hinted, my love. As with the chaperone, he presumed the rest for himself."

She added her laugh to his. "If my acting deserves a place on the stage next to Sarah Siddons, a role beside Edmund Kean surely beckons for you."

Duncan kissed her then straightened the paper in his hands. "Mr Atterlee has sketched us a map showing where the house may be found. I mentioned Armstrong in passing and his residence is several streets distant but with a path that skirts the back of some houses and a field and enables us to make our way there without being noticed should we need to. I'm going to ask Robbie to search out and befriend Armstrong's servants. They will be a mine of information on the comings and goings in the house."

Cairstine looked doubtful. "The upper servants might not oblige."

Duncan shrugged. "I suspect that will depend on how fair a master he is. But either way his housemaids and grooms will be worth a shot."

The carriage slowed and turned carefully between two stone pillars and up a short drive. Cairstine tidied her hair and put her bonnet on straight. "Will I do?" she asked anxiously.

"More than," Duncan assured her as the coach drew up outside a pretty stone-walled house. "Welcome to our temporary abode. I hope it's as good as I have been assured." He waited until the carriage came to a halt and opened the door, thence to get out and help Cairstine alight.

Behind him the large wooden door of the house opened to reveal three males and two females. Their staff.

The sun glinted off the mullioned windows, which sparkled as if to welcome them. To each side of the portico neat rose bushes shared the heady perfume of their blooms.

The overall result was charming.

"Oh my," Cairstine said spontaneously. "How lovely."

The middle male of the three, dressed in the black-tailed suit of his senior position, looked pleased and stepped forwards to bow. "Lord Callander and Lady McColl, welcome. If I may be so bold, I'm Chollerford, your butler. This"—he waved at the taller of the other two men—"is Timothy, who is my able assistant. Alongside me is Mrs Ayton, your cook-housekeeper, Tansy, a maid of all work, and Geordie, the groom of the stables."

The staff named bowed or curtseyed according to their gender. Duncan nodded in acknowledgement and Chollerford cleared his throat.

"May I welcome you both to Denny House, albeit for so brief a time. If I may show you the house?" Duncan glanced at her with a glint in his eye that said, 'Let the next charade begin'.

By the time they had been conducted around the house, Cairstine was relieved to be escorted to her bedchamber. Mrs Ayton had confessed during the tour that she'd prepared a mini feast of local delicacies, which Cairstine's tummy growls couldn't deny would be welcome. Not, however, before she'd indulged in a hot bath.

Duncan had grumbled, while they had been shown around, of how inconvenient it was for Cairstine's lady's maid to have been taken unwell and that the arrival of her chaperone had been delayed until the morrow. Thankfully, Mrs Ayton offered Tansy's services for the dual role in the meantime. The young lass, now elevated to Cairstine's new maid, arranged for a bath to be prepared in double-quick time and the warmth of the water soothed her travel-weary bones.

Tansy held out a towel for her as the bath cooled. "You'll be a prune, my lady, if you don't get out now…and dinner won't be that long. Best get ready."

Cairstine's stomach sounded its agreement. "Has my luggage been brought up?"

Tansy bobbed. "Yes, my lady."

Wrapped in a towel, Cairstine selected a gown of green that matched her eyes and Tansy helped her into it.

As she sat before the dressing table mirror for her hair to be arranged, Cairstine gave thanks to Mrs Ayton's idea. Tansy was excellent, and the style her maid achieved was very flattering. Her hair had been gathered and pinned into a bun on the top of her head. Tendrils of curls escaped from it a soft waterfall and framed her face. She smiled at her reflection. "That's lovely, Tansy. You have some skill in dressing a lady, I think."

The younger girl beamed. "Thank you, my lady. To be lady's maid is my ambition. Me mam was one to the late Mrs Armstrong, before she passed, like."

Cairstine stood up, not at all fazed by the young girl's confessions and refreshing lack of respect for their different stations. It sounded as if she might hear some interesting facts about the Armstrongs if nothing else.

"I believe I've heard mention of the Armstrong family here and there."

Tansy nodded. "You would do, my lady. First family around these parts they are…and me mam's his housekeeper these days. He's away at the moment so I'd not be surprised if Mam doesn't come visiting Aunty Doris tomorrow afternoon. Mrs Ayton, I mean. She's Mam's sister." Her maid blushed. "Sorry, my lady. I've let me mouth get away wi me."

Cairstine offered Tansy a friendly smile and the assurance that her titbits were welcome. "I'm glad for it. To know a little background history of the people here makes me feel not quite such a stranger in a new place. Now if I'm not to upset your aunt, I'd best stir myself and head down for dinner."

* * * *

Duncan pronounced himself quite satisfied after the tour of the house. It was definitely grand enough to be considered the abode of a 'gentleman' and contained all the desired amenities but without unnecessary public rooms such as second and third drawing rooms or a ballroom. The staff seemed an amenable bunch, although if the young maid, Tansy, suited Cairstine in the role of a personal servant, a couple more housemaids wouldn't go amiss. He would consult his wife at dinner.

How he loved those two words.

*My wife.*

He dismissed the butler with his appreciation of all being in order when they reached his bedroom door.

"A very well-run household, Chollerford. I can see us being very comfortable here, thank you. My man will arrive shortly with my curricle. Show him up when he does, will you?"

Chollerford bowed his acknowledgement of the request and Robbie was ushered into Duncan's bedchamber not long after. Duncan smiled when the door closed. "You've done well finding us this house. It's everything I hoped for. My thanks."

"Aye. Well, I can't say the pouch of gold guineas you gave me didn't help. Mr Atterlee's eyes fair lit up when he saw them."

Duncan grinned. "I thought they might. Tomorrow I must engage a proper chaperone. Tansy will do for a lady's maid if Lady Callander likes her, but she hasn't enough years on her for it not to be looked askance at in the other role."

Robbie agreed. "Aye. I caught sight o' the wee lassie lugging a bucket of hot water up the backstairs. She's over young for any more senior position."

Duncan's mood fizzed at being able to properly name his wife out loud, even if he could only do so in private with Robbie, so he did it again. "One good-natured widow coming right up then as a companion to my lady. Now, as to how we proceed so Lady Callander and I can return home in the shortest order, can you think of a way to get to know any of Armstrong's household?"

Robbie frowned as he thought, then offered, "I could maybe pretend to be on the lookout for a livery position and hang around the stables? If the grooms are proud of the bloodstock they care for, they'll be quite happy to stop fer a natter an' show 'em off."

"Good thinking. Now I'd best take a cold-water wash, change into a clean shirt then get on downstairs for dinner."

* * * *

Cairstine was inspecting a small collection of prettily painted miniatures standing on a side table when he entered the room. She looked up and smiled. "A sweet family usually live here by the look of these. I wonder where they are?"

Tansy, back in her role of maid of all work, walked in bearing a covered soup tureen in her hands, followed by the butler. "Abroad, my lady. The master, Mr Griffith, holds a great position in the East India Company. His wife and their children have been able to join him on his travels this time."

She set the first course on the table and Duncan and Cairstine seated themselves to each side of it. Chollerford lifted the lid and served, while Tansy disappeared to fetch more removes. Little conversation could be had above mundane comments on the deliciousness of the food and the pleasant surroundings while the staff were in the room, although with the ghost of a wink Duncan managed to impart one piece of information it would suit them to have passed around the household as gossip.

"So unfortunate for your father not to be able to accompany you south. I do hope he's feeling better."

Cairstine added her mite, "Such a shame his gout should have become inflamed at the same time as my lady's maid, Betsy, was struck down with an attack of dropsy. Luckily, neither is contagious, and it was good of you to step into Papa's place at short notice."

Duncan nearly chuckled. A maid called Betsy didn't exist, nor more than did her dropsy—and Cairstine's father had certainly never suffered from gout. He understood her reasoning though. Their welcome in

Corbridge would be somewhat subdued if word got about that they might have brought an infectious disease with them.

"It was no trouble," he said earnestly. "It suited me to come south and complete some business. I am honoured to have been trusted to safeguard your well-being."

He was convinced Cairstine had trouble keeping her face straight at the pomposity of his words and tone.

"You are the first person Papa thought of," she added as she helped herself to some compote and spooned it delicately into her mouth. "This is delicious, but I vow I am so full." She sighed and yawned. "Would it be possible to stretch our legs before bed? Surely this is a safe place to be out and about before dark on a light summer evening?"

Duncan turned to Chollerford, who stood behind Cairstine's chair to enable her to leave the table.

"Chollerford?"

The man bowed. "The side streets are somewhat less than salubrious, my lord, but if you keep to the main thoroughfare, all will be well. We have a watchman on patrol."

Duncan nodded. "We will remember. Well, my dear, if you so desire... Just a short stroll towards the bridge and back, perhaps, Chollerford?"

"Perfect, if I may say so."

Cairstine stood up. "I'll get my pelisse and be with you directly." She smiled her thanks to the butler and within a few moments had collected her cloak and returned to the hall, where Duncan waited for her.

He murmured as they strolled along the lane towards the seven-arched bridge for which the town was rightly proud. "This would not be possible on a dark night. Or, for that matter, in a place of higher social standing."

"Like Edinburgh or London?"

He nodded. "Here though, it is fine. Now if we stand on the bridge, admire the way the river flows through the arches, then casually pretend to admire the scenery, I believe to our left, we will see Armstrong's house. A grey stone one with an excessive number of chimneys that looks top-heavy, or so Mr Atterlee told me. Evidently Armstrong Senior lives there, and although George has his own estate in the Cheviots, he stays with his father when in Corbridge."

Cairstine leant over the top of the bridge and pointed downwards. "Oh, look, is that a trout?"

"A shadow," Duncan said drily and winked. "The trout will be hiding from the hordes of young boys with their bent wires and string over there." He pointed to the bank where half a dozen or so urchins were perched on the bank below Armstrong's house, which gave them the perfect excuse to look in that direction.

"I do hope they catch some," Cairstine said in a normal tone before lowering her voice. "What now?"

"We go home and go to bed..."

She smirked and peeked up at him "Oh, good—"

"Alone," Duncan added in a level tone. "Sadly."

Cairstine pushed her sense of disappointment to the back of her mind. Duncan had told her men who were aroused and not in a position to sate their needs doused their ardour by way of very cold water. She thought several cold flannels would be required but still shivered at the idea. Duncan glanced at her in concern.

"Cold?"

Cairstine shook her head and admitted the heart of the matter. "Cooling my…self?"

He grinned. "I am the same. However, needs must and hopefully not for long. Now back to Denny House with us and into our solitary bedrooms."

Cairstine smiled. They turned to walk to their temporary home but as they did the germ of an idea occurred. *There is no chaperone as yet.* She nearly giggled but kept her countenance as they sauntered back to Denny House then with maidenly compliance bid Duncan goodnight and requested Tansy to assist her undressing.

Her new lady's maid asked as she entered the bedroom, bearing a jug of warm washing water, "Did you have a pleasant airing, my lady?"

Cairstine summoned a yawn. "I did. It was refreshing but I'm tired now."

Tansy poured the water into the porcelain bowl on the washstand and assisted her to undress. Cairstine refreshed her hands and face then cleaned her teeth before pulling on the night-rail her maid offered her.

The bed was soft and comfortable when she slipped under the covers. She could have easily fallen asleep but requested the night stick be left alight. Tansy bobbed her curtsey and left the room. Cairstine's excitement grew as she counted the minutes until the house became still and silent, then she picked up the candle.

She blew it out as she arrived at Duncan's bedroom door and turned the handle. His breathing, as she'd hoped, was deep and regular. The floorboards didn't creak as she crept towards his bed. She pulled her night-rail up to her waist, slid alongside him, turned onto her side and pressed her bare buttocks into his groin.

He murmured in his sleep, so she wriggled against his hardening crotch. He stirred a little more. "Wh...what...?"

Duncan's cock was awake even if he wasn't. Cairstine took his hand and urged it towards the throbbing nub between her legs.

He groaned, deep and low, when his fingers found her wet muff. "Oh, God... Cairstine..."

"Sssh... No words... Take me..."

He needed no second urging and replaced his fingers with his cockhead. Cairstine pushed her face into the pillow to smother her moan of pleasure as he entered her and began to thrust, hard and urgent. She moved her pelvis in time to his rhythm, her buttocks grinding on his groin as the joy of their climax built. Waves of orgasm spread from the centre of her muff, through her belly and down her thighs. A mewl escaped her mouth. Duncan thrust faster, then tensed, his breath hissing through his teeth.

He put his arms around her and held her close. Cairstine relaxed. Duncan's body warm against her own was heavenly, but it would be far too easy to drift off to sleep, so she kissed his lips and whispered, "I love you." Then she slipped out of his bed and left the room as silently as she'd arrived.

* * * *

Cairstine felt bright-eyed and bushy-tailed when she tripped downstairs for breakfast in the morning. The glint in Duncan's eye told her he felt the same way.

"Sleep well?" she teased as Mrs Ayton bustled in with a plate of kidneys, followed by Tansy with a jug of hot chocolate.

Duncan glanced at the chocolate and shuddered then nodded his thanks to Chollerford when the butler put a mug of ale by his plate. "Very much better after a little late-night refreshment, thank you."

Cairstine smothered a grin and glanced down at her plate, lest the staff notice the byplay. "A most excellent aid to restful repose then."

The servants left the room, no doubt to attend to other duties such as making the beds, there not being a full complement of staff, which gave them a few minutes' leeway for private conversation.

Cairstine picked up her teacup. "What are our plans for today?"

"I thought a walk into town to call on Mr Atterlee and enquire whether he could recommend a suitable candidate to be your chaperone?"

The thought was not appealing. It was very much more comfortable without one. But their visit to Corbridge was business, not pleasure, and the illusion they were presenting had to be maintained. Cairstine nodded. "Then perhaps a general saunter to get our bearings?"

Duncan agreed. "Yes, we should appear to show some interest in the town that you're supposedly considering making your home. Best not push our luck, though. A brief stroll after dinner is one thing, an outing another. Ask Tansy to accompany you."

Cairstine nodded, finished her bowl of oatmeal and ran upstairs to find her bonnet. Her maid was restoring order to her bedroom and her face lit up when Cairstine made her request.

"A walk in the sunshine compared to scrubbing the kitchen floor? I should like that very much. Thank you, my lady."

Cairstine smiled. "Run along then and tidy your hair under a clean cap. I'll see you by the front door in ten minutes."

"Too right you will," Tansy assured her and trotted from the room.

Cairstine watched her go, then put on her bonnet and tied its ribbons under her chin. A pair of white kid gloves and a reticule dangling from her wrist completed her ensemble. Both Duncan and Tansy waited downstairs in the hall and the day was beautifully warm and sunny when Chollerford opened the door and bowed them out onto the street.

Cairstine walked alongside Duncan with her maid following two paces behind her—the three of them presenting a perfect picture of respectability. The flagstones underfoot were agreeably flat and even to walk on, the cobbles of the road freshly swept and the houses lining it well-maintained. Corbridge, as Papa's guidebook had indicated, was indeed a prosperous and tidy place.

Duncan led the way with surety and a twinkle in his eye. "I took directions from Robbie while you were fetching your bonnet. He's off on an outing of his own today."

Cairstine glanced up at him curiously and he smiled. "Making enquires here and there as to the availability of any bloodstock."

She immediately understood his guarded reference. 'Here and there' was Armstrong's house, or rather, his stables. A left turn followed by a right, three streets later the properties changed from residential to smaller bow-windowed houses, the gold lettering on the glass indicating the business district had been reached. Duncan opened the door inscribed with Mr Atterlee's name and Cairstine looked around at a neat but paper-musty office. A clerk sat at his desk looked up when he saw them. Duncan handed him his card and he jumped to his feet after he read the name and title printed on it. "Yes, your lordship. Right away, your lordship. Of course."

Tansy was offered a chair in the clerk's room and they were escorted into the solicitor's inner sanctum not two minutes later. Portly as described, Mr Atterlee bowed. "My lord, I'm honoured. Would you and the young lady care to take a seat?"

Duncan waited for Cairstine to sit then did so himself and made the introduction. "The Lady Cairstine McColl. As I mentioned previously, her father, the duke, is unwell, so I have undertaken to escort her."

If Mr Atterlee had hoped for any further details as to the reason why the Lady Cairstine McColl might be travelling south, he was doomed to disappointment as Duncan moved swiftly on. "We require a chaperone. Could you recommend a lady suitable for the position?"

Mr Atterlee smiled, his face genial and kind. "Indeed, I can. A widow of my acquaintance, Mrs Evanna Percival-Smyth. Her husband, God rest his soul, departed this earth three years ago, and unfortunately, without the blessing of offspring, his estate passed to a distant cousin…"

The solicitor's mouth puckered into a moue of distaste. "The inheritor declined to make any provision for the bereaved widow other than the bare minimum, so she has taken a lease on a house in town to accommodate boarders attending Dame Fortesque's Academy for Young Ladies. The school is closed for the summer at present. The boarders have returned from whence they came for a few weeks, leaving Mrs Percival-Smyth free to accommodate your request and welcoming of the additional income offered."

A genteel lady down on her luck. If it helped the lady, and she appeared to be the sort of person she could get on with, Cairstine was agreeable.

Duncan glanced at her and she gave him a slight nod. He smiled at Mr Atterlee. "Excellent. Perhaps the lady concerned would care to call at Denny House and take tea with us this afternoon? Around four?"

Mr Atterlee looked both pleased and relieved. "I'm sure she would be delighted to come. I'll send a note straight round to inform her of her good fortune."

# Chapter Ten

"I see the necessity, but I can't say I relish the idea," Cairstine admitted after Mr Atterlee had escorted them out.

Duncan offered Cairstine his arm and Tansy took her place behind them. "I know—but if the lady is a well-established part of the community, who knows what titbits about the Armstrongs you will discover from being in her company?"

She smiled up at him. "I hadn't thought of that."

They walked on in perfect harmony. It was a warm but not overly hot day. Perfect for strolling around the town.

Duncan steered her across the road, dodged a pie-carrying urchin and another being towed by a dog almost as big as himself. A cultivated green space came into view. He lowered his voice to be out of Tansy's hearing when they turned down a side street and suggested, "If we stroll towards the park, just before the gates discover a stone in your shoe? We can have another glance towards Armstrong's house while I remove it."

Cairstine obliged and together they surveyed the layout of the property. Neat gardens led to the riverside. The back of the house displayed a fine stone terrace to stroll upon should the weather prove clement.

"The front entrance must be street side," Duncan muttered. "Still, until the Merry Widow calls on us there is little more we can accomplish so, have you any preference to fill our time?"

Cairstine peered at him speculatively and he laughed.

"Apart from that."

"Spoilsport," she retorted. "Maybe we could go for a short drive? I have read that there is a small physic garden not far away, just across the river. It doesn't really open to the public apparently..."

She paused for effect. "Except for locals, which we are."

Duncan laughed. "That we are. Then we will head there and see if we count as acceptable visitors."

An hour later they tooled down the lane, which Cairstine had read on a leaflet she'd found in the house led to Long Layers, the house where the garden was. She lifted her head to the sunshine. "How I love this. I can almost forget why we are here."

Duncan glanced at her. "You'll get freckles."

"I have freckles, as well you know."

"I do," he said appreciatively. "In some very interesting places."

She blushed. "Du...nc...an."

He laughed. "I couldn't resist." He slowed the horse to a gentle walk. "Ah, we have arrived at our destination, I believe. Let's see if we can rouse someone." He eyed the closed gates with disfavour. "It doesn't look very promising."

* * * *

"Closed," Cairstine said in disgust as ten minutes later they retraced their steps. "The family have gone south this morning. *This* morning of all things. How unlucky is that? And to say as we were *unknown* we could not be admitted. Did they think we were going to do something nefarious? Steal the belladonna or uproot the poppies?"

Duncan bit his lip so as not to chuckle at her outraged expression. "I'm sure it's not quite that bad. However, think about it from their point of view. Would you want persons unknown to have free range around your property when you have the sorts of plants they have?"

"I suppose not," Cairstine said grudgingly. "But it is a shame."

"Yes, my love, but the gateman did say they will be back in a sennight, so if we are still in Corbridge we will try again. Meanwhile we have had a pleasant drive, forgotten our cares for a while and are heading back to see if your prospective companion suits."

Cairstine frowned. "If she does, how will we explain it could only be for a few days? It seems a little underhanded to keep that from her."

He agreed and considered the matter. "We will say we are not sure how long we will be here, or if she will be needed to travel on with us, but that we will pay her the full rate until her boarders return."

She smiled. "That sounds perfect."

Duncan urged the horse to a faster gait. "Then let's get back and wait for Mrs Percival-Smyth."

* * * *

Robbie had returned from his foray to the Armstrong stables and was making himself useful in those belonging to Denny House when they returned. Wishing to hear what, if anything, Robbie had discovered, Duncan handed the reins to Geordie and nodded to Robbie to follow them inside.

Cairstine ran upstairs to tidy her hair before their afternoon visitor arrived and the men made their way to Duncan's room where their conversation would not be overheard.

"So, what news?" he asked when Robbie shut the door behind them.

"Aye… Well…" Robbie frowned. "The grooms were friendly enough once they realised I knew my horseflesh but…"

He hesitated as if searching for the right words, so Duncan encouraged him on. "And…?"

"They were odd. Their master has a distrust of strangers apparently. Especially if he finds one on his property…"

"As many property owners do."

"Aye. But it was more than that. Glancing over their shoulders while we was chatting. All twitchy like. It's a town stable. As near street side as could be considered on public view. I hadn't trespassed onto private land but they was more nervous than you would expect to find as a casual passer-by who'd just stopped to share a comment or two on an old hack and a couple of carriage horses."

It appeared that whatever the cause, Armstrong Senior was definitely an eccentric of the first order. Duncan stored away the nugget for when they met the man in person. He thanked Robbie, straightened his cravat and went to see if Cairstine was ready to descend to the drawing room and await their guest.

* * * *

A soft tap sounded on the door. Cairstine motioned for Tansy to open it. Duncan stood outside her room and his lips twitched as he glanced at her. "Are you ready?"

She nodded, joined him and waited for the door to close before narrowing her eyes at him. "Oh, yes. And what exactly is amusing you?"

He grinned down at her. "You looking so prim and proper, so demure, so *not* my feisty lady-love. You appear as if nothing untoward would ever dare happen to you."

Cairstine stuck her nose in the air. "Exactly. First appearances can be deceptive, and I do not want to put Mrs Percival-Smyth off if she is at all suitable. Let her find out my demure appearance is just a façade for my real self. By then I can hope it will be too late for her to renege on her promise if she wants to. *If,* of course, she is suitable."

"Not long now until you find out, it wants but five minutes to the hour."

Chollerford showed the lady concerned into the sitting room at a few minutes past the appointed time and Cairstine decided she liked the look of her immediately. Mrs Percival-Smyth's face positively exuded good nature. The bow of her lips tilted upwards to hint that a smile was her habitual expression, and her brow was smooth, without frown lines. The impression of her being a person she would get on with very well was cemented when their guest dispensed with the tiresome formalities of who should curtsey to whom and instead offered out her hand.

"Mrs Percival-Smyth. Pleased to meet you."

In turn, they shook her hand, then Duncan invited her to be seated while Cairstine nodded to Chollerford – the sign the tea tray was required.

Tansy brought it into the room and Cairstine offered an opening overture of friendship by giving precedence to her older, once-married guest, despite her own superior title. "Would you care to pour?"

Mrs Percival-Smyth looked delighted. "Indeed, I would be honoured to do so."

Tansy took her cue and placed the laden tray on the rosewood occasional table in front of Mrs Percival-Smyth's chair. Their guest exhibited she knew the etiquette of the tea ceremony very well by pouring tea into the delicate porcelain cups that, unlike china of lesser quality, would not shatter for her doing so, and only then enquired as to their preference for milk or sugar to be added.

Tansy hovered and passed the filled cups, balanced on their saucers, before bobbing her curtsey and following Chollerford from the room. Duncan had accepted one small sugar lump and stirred his tea to encourage it to dissolve. "So, Mrs Percival-Smyth. You see how we are situated. Do you feel you could come and stay for a short time to lend us your countenance?"

"Well, I could…" Their guest sipped her tea. "On one condition…"

Cairstine held her breath. Duncan sat straighter.

Mrs Percival-Smyth gave her the ghost of a wink. "That I can be Mrs P when we're together informally? Percival-Smyth is such a mouthful. One of my boarders, a cheeky minx, shortened it when funning one day, and I like it. I've been Mrs P to my lovely young ladies ever since."

Cairstine giggled. "So long as I can be Lady C?"

Mrs P's brown eyes twinkled. "Not M for McColl?"

Cairstine couldn't resist giving Duncan the briefest hint of a smirk. "Lady C will suit me very well."

Duncan set his cup and saucer on the table and stood. "I see I'm superfluous, so with your leave, ladies, I'll head off to attend to some business and let you two decide on the details."

Cairstine watched the door close behind him then suggested, "Would you care to see the available bedrooms? D…ah…Lord Callander selected one on the street side but for myself, I preferred a room overlooking the gardens."

To Cairstine's relief, Mrs P didn't seem to notice her small stumble and subsequent correction of her words. She nodded towards the side console table on which the miniatures of the Denny family were displayed and smiled. "I must admit Denny House is familiar to me, although not the rooms upstairs. Two of their daughters attend the Academy as day pupils and I have been an invited to take tea here on several occasions."

Whether it was Mrs P calling attention to the painted likenesses or her turning her head away from the sunshine flooding the room and into the shadow of a side-on profile that jogged her memory Cairstine couldn't tell, but…

*Papa's study. The framed silhouette he keeps tucked away in his desk drawer. It was Mama when young, surely…?*

"Ah... It was such a shame my father was taken ill and couldn't accompany me to Corbridge. I don't suppose you're acquainted with him?"

Mrs P waved an airy hand. "Yes...but, oh my goodness...so many years ago during my one and only winter in Edinburgh. Not a proper season, but we treated it as one. We bumped into each other here and there at various soirees about the Town. I don't suppose I'd even recognise him now, or he me, should we walk past each other on the street."

"So, he wouldn't have a likeness of you? A silhouette in profile?"

Mrs P smiled, although that was not the emotion reflected in her eyes. "No. I can't imagine why he would. Shall we view the bedrooms?"

Cairstine led the way from the room. It would be rude to pursue the subject in the face of Mrs P shutting it down, but it niggled at her mind. There had been flash of what looked like pain in those kind brown eyes and she couldn't help but wonder what could have caused it.

Her new companion chose the bedroom beside Cairstine's own and it was such a pretty room Cairstine couldn't blame her, although it would put paid to any midnight outings to Duncan's bed. The walls were too thin and the floorboards too squeaky for it not to be noticed. She left her there to settle in and was careful to play her part of a demure young miss over dinner, but even so, the Merry Widow's eyes seemed to contain a knowing twinkle whenever she surveyed herself and Duncan.

Attendance at church for the Sunday service in the morning was pronounced *de rigueur*. *All* of Corbridge who were important would be there, and as that should include Armstrong Senior, Cairstine acquiesced with perfect acceptance.

* * * *

Duncan tossed uncomfortably in his bed. With a chaperone on the premises there would be no surprise visit from his wife. Damn it! Still, the arrival of Mrs Percival-Smyth had moved their plans forwards and with that thought to comfort him he fell into an uneasy sleep.

The morning dawned fair and warm and, once dressed, he waited in the front hall for the ladies to descend. They were not long in joining him and he contemplated the age-old dilemma as he followed them out of the front door. With two ladies to escort, should he offer each an arm, or would they prefer to walk together while he followed behind, and if it was the former which of the ladies should be on the less-favoured roadside? The choice was made by the generous width of the pavement and Mrs P, with a self-deprecating smile, laying her right hand on his offered forearm while clasping her parasol handle with the other. "I'm naturally left-handed, I'm afraid."

Duncan thought back to dinner the previous evening. "I wouldn't have guessed."

"No. As a child my governess tied my left arm to my side in an effort to correct the fault. I can use the silverware when sitting to table in a satisfactorily normal manner but other than that her endeavours failed."

"To restrain your movements seems unnecessarily harsh," Cairstine objected.

Mrs P's smile softened. "My father, the silly man, even had me Christened Evanna, which means right-handed, in an attempt to escape the family jinx—I'm a Kerr from the borders—but it was not to be. My left hand remains stubbornly dominant, such bad form when I offer my hand in greeting or if dining. Do you mind?"

A Kerr. Cairstine had heard of those left-handed Border Reivers. They even had the stairs in their castle spiralling in the opposite direction to the norm, to allow them to have their sword hand free. All the better to repel invaders.

"It doesn't bother me at all," Cairstine assured her. "I feel sorry for those of you who have been forced to use the other hand though. That cannot be easy."

"That's the truth. Plus it used to be said if you were *caurie*-fisted you were a witch. Not a healthy reputation to have in days not that long gone."

"Then let's hope the witch bit might put fear of God into anyone who wants to do us harm and give thanks we are more open-minded these days."

The church bells rang out, summoning parishioners to service, as they arrived at the lynch gate that guarded the entrance to the churchyard. Duncan held it open for the ladies to precede him, and Cairstine took the chance to murmur, "If we sit near the back, I'll ask Mrs P to name the local worthies when they walk past us to take their seats."

He nodded. "Good idea. With the Armstrongs being the foremost family in town, I'll wager they'll have their own pew at the head of the congregation. Take heed, love, the service may well be different from that in a kirk. Copy Mrs P for how to go on."

By the brief flash of worry that crossed her face, Duncan could tell Cairstine hadn't thought of that and he noticed she crossed her fingers. No doubt in hope she'd not draw attention to herself by doing something untoward. She pasted her most demure expression onto her face, which nearly made him chuckle, as did her eyes watering when they stepped into the nave and encountered a cloud of incense being wafted over all entering the holy space by a surpliced lay-server.

Observing the ancient architectural features reminiscent of Saxon and Norman masonry surrounding them, Duncan suspected the service would be conducted according to the elaborate ritual commonly known south of the border as 'high church'.

Mrs P did as Cairstine had requested, and in soft voice duly identified all those making their way down the aisle until at last Duncan heard the name they had been waiting for. He sat a little straighter but kept his gaze casual as he caught sight of the man who had brought them to Corbridge. A tall but slight figure that to Duncan's eyes seemed stooped and somewhat withered, as if age had caught up with what at one time would have been a much more imposing figure of a man. That Armstrong wore an old-fashioned white half-periwig of the type still favoured by gentlemen of an age similar to that of poor mad King George didn't help matters, especially when it wobbled on his head each time its owner nodded to an acquaintance in the congregation. Beside him he felt Cairstine's shoulders shake at what seemed the inevitable descent of the wig to the floor, however, to give Armstrong's valet his due, the precariously balanced object managed to stay on its owner's head.

The service proceeded and he and Cairstine mirrored Mrs P's movements for when to sit and stand and kneel to pray. They mouthed the responses, not knowing the correct wording of a Church of England-sung Eucharist, and nobody seemed to notice that they had. He nudged Cairstine when nearly two hours later they were released from their aching knees—the hassocks were not exactly soft—and the vicar made his way to the church door to bid his congregation farewell. "Make an excuse to loiter outside in the churchyard until Armstrong appears and I'll give Mrs P the nod to make the introduction."

"I'll do my best."

Duncan nodded briefly. "Here we go."

The sun had climbed high in a cloudless sky during the time they had been in the dim, cool interior of the church. Cairstine discovered a conveniently loosened sandal as they stepped outside and paused to adjust it. Mrs P handed Duncan her parasol to hold over the both of them while she stood in front of Cairstine with her skirts slightly spread to protect any onlooker from the shocking sight of an exposed ankle.

Cairstine straightened when Armstrong's bewigged head appeared. "There. All fixed. Such a nuisance, but it would have been impossible to continue on our way home as it was. It would have broken and blistered my skin."

Duncan looked pointedly at Mrs P then indicated Armstrong with a nod. Mrs P took his meaning and sent a beaming smile in Armstrong's direction.

He left the company he was talking to and made his way directly to them. "Mrs Percival-Smyth, how delightful to see you this fine morning. And in the company of Corbridge's newest residents, if I'm not mistaken?" He turned towards Duncan. "I heard tell that Denny House had been leased. By yourself, sir?"

Mrs P curtseyed and corrected that misnomer immediately. "That it has. By the Earl of Callander and his ward, the Lady Cairstine McColl."

Armstrong's eyes widened. That he was surprised to hear those names was evident on his face. "Well, well. You don't say. My apologies, my lord. I had no knowledge I was in the presence of nobility. Gordon Armstrong at your service."

Armstrong's blue eyes appeared guileless, but Duncan was not about to take that at face value. "Were you not expecting to see Lady McColl in Corbridge, sir?"

He had been right not to do so. A gleam appeared that could have been a sign of pleasure but could equally well be taken for gleeful smugness. "Maybe, but maybe not like this, without due notice. However, you're here now, so you'd best come to dinner this evening." He gave Mrs P a dismissive glance. "Suppose you'll have to come as well."

Mrs P declined to curtsey in the face of such a back-handed invitation. "Thank you for such a charming offer, but…"

Duncan gave her a warning glance. She shut her mouth with an audible snap.

Cairstine stiffened. Her hand twitched but she held her tongue. Duncan flicked a nonexistent speck of lint from his sleeve in a bored manner and assumed his aristocratic drawl. "As you say. No need to dally. My ward, her chaperone and I will be with you at six o'clock sharp. Do not keep me waiting. I dislike it. Until then."

He turned on his heel, offered each lady an arm apiece, and they walked away with Cairstine hissing through gritted teeth. "I hate him already. So rude! Has he no manners?"

If Mrs P heard his wife's angry words, she made no mention of them, but instead, smiled serenely. "Well, an invitation to dinner. How lovely." Her tone made it sound anything but. "What shall you wear, Lady C? For myself, I have a pale blue satin that I declare has not had an airing this summer. Will there be other company, do you suppose? If so, evening gloves will be required..."

Cairstine's stance relaxed under Mrs P's inconsequential but soothing chatter. "I have a leaf-green gown that suits my colouring very well."

"Yes. That it would. Shades of gold would also be becoming on you, I believe..."

# Chapter Eleven

Cairstine shot Duncan a glance before she ran up the stairs to her room at Denny House. *We need to talk.*

Mrs P loosened the bonnet ribbons tied under her chin and remarked as she followed Cairstine up at a more sedate pace. "I will see you anon, my love. I need to get myself in a good frame of mind to cope with Armstrong Senior. He is very trying."

That was all Cairstine needed to hear.

Tansy was thankfully absent from her room when Cairstine entered it. She resisted the urge to give the door an almighty slam behind her but did stamp her feet to relieve a measure of pent-up temper. "Trying, is he? I'll give him trying. Here now, am I? Best come to dinner then, had I? What an insufferable pig!"

There was a tap at the door. Presuming it was Tansy, she called, "Come."

It wasn't. Mrs P's voice sounded from the other side of it, "You'll have to open it to admit me, Lady C. My hands are full."

Intrigued, Cairstine did so and saw Mrs P holding a stemmed glass in each hand, both filled to the brim with a pale liquid. "Sherry," she said, handing one over. "Marvellous stuff. A real antidote against someone who's getting on your very last nerve."

"You're a mind reader. Take a seat and let's moan together for a while."

Mrs P settled herself in the soft, chintz-covered fireside chair, sipped and looked at Cairstine expectantly. "So… Gordon Armstrong? He didn't recognise your face as such, although he certainly knew *who* you are. How are you acquainted with him? And why accept an invitation to dine with a man you so evidently dislike? Surely you could have cried off? Or your guardian could, being the higher peer? If I have overstepped the mark, please say so. I will not be offended." She grinned and appeared twenty years younger. "Disappointed, I allow, but I would not take umbrage. I do tend to be somewhat outspoken, and I accept it does not suit everyone."

Cairstine could *not* be offended by her blunt questions. Mrs P's brown eyes held caring, compassion, not nosiness. She perched on the footstool and swallowed a mouthful of her drink, which warmed her throat as it slid down. There was something she found intrinsically trustworthy about her companion and it would be a relief to confide in an older, more experienced woman—someone like the mother she no longer had.

She sipped again. "I've never met the man before today, nor he me, but I'm here to marry his son, George." She grimaced. "Or so he believes."

Mrs P's eyes searched her face. "And why would you do that?"

Cairstine considered how best to frame her reply. *Straightforward and to the point.* "The Armstrongs, definitely the elder, and maybe the pair of them in collusion, are blackmailing my father."

Mrs P's lips thinned and her face whitened. "How so?"

"They've obtained a document. A piece of family history with the potential to ruin him..."

"And therefore, you also?" Mrs P queried. "The *cads*."

Cairstine lifted her chin. "The Armstrongs can do their damnedest, and I will stand alongside my father with my head held high. I'll pretend to entertain the thought of George as a prospective husband in order to search for the document mentioned, but there will be no marriage."

Mrs P smiled. "That is good." She hesitated for a second. "However, I hope you don't mind me adding my mite here. Looking after my young ladies as I do for most of the year, I'm possibly a little more perceptive than many. Forgive my noticing, and I hope I'm not speaking out of turn, but I believe the Earl of Callander is in love with you and he wishes you for his wife." She patted Cairstine's arm. "This is another time you can tell me to mind my own business, but I do hope you won't. I am on your side."

Cairstine saw no reason not to admit the truth of the matter. "Yes, we are in love but there is more to it than that. I am already his wife. We handfasted before coming south, but we keep that fact between ourselves and our witness so we can do whatever we may, short of my committing bigamy, to save Papa."

Mrs P slapped her hands on her thighs and her ample bosoms jiggled as she chuckled. "I thought there was more to all this than meets the eye. Good for you. It's a brave action to defy convention. Not many young ladies of your age would dare to do so. I wish I… But enough of that." She leant forwards and spoke in a soft, confidential voice, "Gordon Armstrong is a very strange man. It wouldn't surprise me to find him an aficionado of the poppy." She closed one eyelid briefly. "Not that you heard that from me."

Cairstine gasped. Would that be a help or a hindrance to their cause? She vowed to impart the information to Duncan at the earliest opportunity. "My lips are sealed," she asserted. "Except for sharing that titbit with my husband. Every little snippet of information might be vital."

"I'd expect no less. Men can be confounded nuisances at times, but at others they have their uses. This is one of them in my mind. You can count on my assistance, both of you, as and how you need it. Diversionary tactics or whatever. I will undertake to aid you, just ask."

"Thank you. My papa doesn't deserve any of this. He's a good man."

Mrs P set down her glass and stood.

"I can agree with you there." She sighed and appeared so desolate Cairstine was taken aback. Before Cairstine had to time to do or say anything, Mrs P visibly pulled herself together. "I disappointed him once. He invited me somewhere I didn't have courage to attend." She shook her skirts out briskly as if that would lift her mood. "Ah well, it was many years ago, and as they say is water under the bridge. I would wager he would hardly remember it, or me, now. However, it would comfort me to know I've assisted his cause in any small way I can. And now, my dear, you should ring for Tansy if we are to be changed into our finery in time for dinner at six."

Cairstine glanced at the clock and gave a small yelp of horror. "Oh, my yes." On an impulse she hugged Mrs P, who immediately returned the gesture. "Thank you," Cairstine said. "I am so pleased it was you who was suggested to be my chaperone."

"There, there." Mrs P patted her shoulder. "No more than I. Now by your leave I'll go and make myself presentable. I might not like the blessed man, but I'm not going to be anything other than at my best and gracious, even if I do have to bite my tongue. Between us we shall appear as models of compliance and not at the type of females that will take our chance to snoop around the wretched man's house should the opportunity arise."

Cairstine laughed. "The ladies' excuse-me it is then."

She rang for Tansy, dressed quickly and managed a few minutes' conversation with Duncan to relay what had passed between herself and Mrs P before the lady herself joined them in the hall. The front door was opened and they stepped outside. "The carriage? For such a short journey?" Cairstine asked.

"We are, my love," Duncan said as he handed both her and Mrs P into the carriage, "going to arrive as befits my station. As you know, I can appear very autocratic if needs be. I suspect Gordon Armstrong to be the type of man who toadies to those he perceives to be his superiors and browbeat others he considers beneath him…"

He took his seat, gave Robbie the signal for the horses to move off then continued.

"Armstrong's smug attitude in the churchyard leads me to think, if he is not the instigator of this scheme, he is fully conversant and in agreement with it. He may believe he has Cairstine's father over a barrel, but he will find me a tougher proposition altogether. I expect him to broach the subject at some point during the evening and I shall try to rile him by appearing uninterested, as if both he and his son are beneath my notice. If I've read his character correctly, I think he will admit more than he should to prove he is not a man to be so disregarded."

"You'll do the supercilious look-down-your-nose thing?" Cairstine smiled. "The one you do so well?"

Duncan inclined his head and did indeed look down his nose at her.

Mrs P chuckled. "Perfect. That should rile him."

Cairstine clapped her hands. "Oh, very good."

Mrs P nodded. "You've summed Armstrong up perfectly, my lord. On one hand, a first-class snob, on the other a blustering bully."

"Mrs P and I are intending to perform the ladies' excuse-me at some point this evening. Perhaps he'll take the chance to broach the subject with you while we are absent."

"I'll give him every encouragement to do so," Duncan assured her.

"Keep him talking for as long as you can," Cairstine suggested. "So Mrs P and I can take a quick snoop around the place."

Duncan nodded and their carriage lurched to a halt. The door was flung open by a liveried footman.

"Liveried?" Cairstine whispered to Mrs P.

"Delusions of grandeur," Mrs P whispered back. "Which means it will be perfectly acceptable for me to accompany you to the withdrawing room once we have eaten. To, ah, freshen up."

Cairstine grinned her agreement, then gave her hand to a waiting Duncan and stepped out onto the pebbled drive.

"How charming." The words were spontaneous as she looked closely at the ivy-clad building. From the road this side of the house was unseen, and presented a much prettier picture than the plain austere walls she had noticed before.

"Ah, you know a good thing when you see it, eh? Perfect place to live, eh?" Gordon Armstrong had approached unobserved by Cairstine. "Snug house, eh?" His eyes appeared glazed as he stared at her and nodded meaningfully. "Just needs a mistress, eh?"

*If he says 'eh' once more I might scream. That would show him what a termagant I could be...eh?* Perhaps it was just as well she didn't articulate that sentence. Cairstine tried to emulate the way Duncan peered down his nose.

"I have no idea, sir, but perhaps one day a lady might agree." It was as near as she dared go without openly disagreeing, or being rude. "For myself, I'm content as I am, but I can't help but admire the façade."

If Armstrong understood her double entendre he didn't show it. "Then let's hope you're as happy with your dinner, eh? Come on in, your lordship, my lady, ah, er, Mrs Percival-Smyth, there's a pre-dinner decanter awaiting."

He turned to Duncan. "No doubt you'll approve of it. If I say so myself it's the best Madeira you'll find hereabouts. My son would have it no other way." He guffawed loudly. "Not that I'd let him."

* * * *

Somehow Duncan doubted it would be Armstrong's first alcoholic refreshment of the day when they were shown into a drawing room, the sideboard of which groaned with bottles of every shape and size. Their host paused in front of it and puffed out his chest.

"Now, I have decanters of Madeira or canary wine for the ladies, but for you and I, my lord, perhaps a fine whisky, ten years in the barrel, or I have a cognac recently arrived from France?"

Duncan raised his eyes briefly heavenward and replied in a bored drawl, "Not hard spirits before dinner, my good man. A small sherry will suffice if you have one."

Gordon Armstrong looked disappointed but hurried to make amends. "Of course, of course. What was I thinking of, eh? Dooley, pour the drinks." The footman stepped forwards as they took their seats. The ladies sat side by side on a two-seater sofa, himself and George Armstrong in an armchair apiece each side of the fireplace. He accepted his drink and was impressed when Cairstine didn't even bristle when presented with half a glass of canary wine that Armstrong deemed suitable for 'the young lady'. It turned out to be the only courtesy he directed towards his female guests before dinner, although he topped his glass up twice before the door was flung open and a very staid butler announced, in stentorian tones, that dinner was served.

Without a backwards look, Armstrong rushed from the room. Duncan glanced at Cairstine, then Mrs P. "Ladies, may I offer you an arm?"

"What a perfectly odious toad," Cairstine said under her breath as she laid her hand on his forearm.

"I am so looking forward to that man getting his comeuppance," Mrs P muttered through gritted teeth as she took Duncan's other arm.

Duncan nodded grimly. "Hold fast and let's keep a united front, ladies."

Three abreast they walked into the dining room where Armstrong was already seated at the head of a table that could have seated a dozen, but had places laid for four at one end. His bright-blue gaze held no hint that he'd just committed a major social *faux pas.* "Come along. Come along. Sit yourselves down, eh. Can't have the food getting cold, eh."

Duncan escorted the ladies to their places before taking his own. The footman, Dooley, appeared at Armstrong's shoulder with a tumbler of water and a small glass bottle on a silver tray. "Your medicinal, sir?"

Armstrong's irises brightened further at the sight. "Yes, yes. Seven drops, Dooley. That's the way, eh."

While he drank, Cairstine took the chance to widen her eyes and mouth at Duncan, *Laudanum* and *strong spirits*?

He returned an imperceptible nod. *I'm afraid so.*

His fears that under that particular combination their host would become totally addled were confirmed when the food was served. The man, with his mouth full, chose that moment to speak. He stared at Duncan with a sly expression.

"So, my lord. Shall we have ourselves a merry little marriage? I presume you've been sent here to hand over the dowry, set the date and whatnot. Shame George isn't here. But no matter, eh? He'll be back soon enough." He turned his bright-blue gaze towards Cairstine and winked. "Don't you worry yourself, little miss. Your bridegroom won't be missing from the altar on the big day."

Cairstine half-rose in her seat. If looks could have killed, Gordon Armstrong would have been a smoking pile on the floor. Duncan kicked her leg under the table. She sat back down and nudged Mrs P, who patted her lips with her serviette and laid it carefully down on the table next to her plate.

"Delicious, thank you. Ah, I hate to be indelicate, but...er...the facilities?" She gave a very good imitation of a simper. "Not to be discussed in polite circles, I know, but ah..." She let her voice trail off.

Armstrong stared at her owlishly, as if her words were beyond his comprehension. "What's that? Eh?"

Cairstine took up the plea. "Sir, the ladies' withdrawing room, if you please."

The footman bent and spoke softly into Armstrong's ear, after which Armstrong cackled. "Go and show 'em then, Dooley. Ladies, eh? Can't hold their victuals, eh?" He waved vaguely in the direction of the door then looked at Duncan. "Tell you what. We'll have a port while they're away. A proper end to a meal, eh?"

Duncan resigned himself to an unpleasant half-hour and replied equably, "As you suggest, sir." He silently wished Cairstine and Mrs P good luck in their endeavours and began his own attempt to pump Armstrong for information as they left the room. "So, the prospective bridegroom. Where is he exactly?"

# Chapter Twelve

"The man is deranged, surely?" Cairstine whispered to Mrs P as they followed the footman down a long, dimly lit corridor.

Mrs P nodded and, with a swift glance to the footman, who was several paces ahead, spoke out of the side of her mouth. "Much as he plotted for it, I suspect your appearing in Corbridge at short notice has made him nervous. He's obviously overindulged this evening, which might work to our advantage."

Cairstine nodded and with one eye on the man ahead artlessly nudged the nearest door so it was a few more inches open. To her disappointment, all she could see were holland covers, ghostly in the moonlight that showed through the un-shuttered window. Not a room that was currently in use. The next room was no different.

The footman stopped, opened a door and took a step back.

"The withdrawing room, ladies." He beckoned to a young page stood farther up the hallway. "I must return. Boy, show the ladies back to the dining room."

The lad grinned when Dooley was out of sight. "And if I may be so bold, Mrs P. It'll not be what you are used to, I'll be bound."

Mrs P took a long look at his freckled face and smiled. "Sydney Coperstine, I didn't recognise you for minute. So smart as you are in your velvet waistcoat and knee breeches. What are you doing here and not on your pa's farm?"

"Not enough work, or space, ma'am, what with our Ben bringing home his Annie, and them having a bairn, so I came here. Not for long though, not if I can help it. The master's mean-spirited and halfway to being mad, I reckon. Last night he were sat with a chamber pot on his head."

Cairstine giggled and hid a grin behind her gloved hand. Sydney glanced at her. "It were clean, but even so. I ain't wanting to stay."

"I don't blame you, nor would I. I'll keep my ears open," Mrs P promised. "Sydney, where would he keep letters and documents he didn't want anyone to find?"

He nodded towards one of the closed doors. "In 'is desk, I'd wager. In t'study. But it's locked. He's allus saying the future's in there and his George better know it and do what's good for 'im. I'd not want to be George Armstrong for all the jewels in the crown." He paused. "Are you needin' in?"

"He has something belonging to my papa," Cairstine said. "It may be in there."

"That don't surprise me. If you have an 'atpin or an 'air grip I'll get you in."

Cairstine took a hairgrip from the loose chignon that Tansy had created. "My hair should still stay in place."

Sydney took it and applied himself to the lock. Within seconds he held the door open. "In you go, I'll keep watch."

"Sydney Coperstine, you will not," Mrs P said firmly. "You need this job for now. Go back and say we said we'll make our own way back. If necessary, I'll say we got lost." She flapped her hands at him. "Now shoo."

Sydney nodded with obvious reluctance. "Well, all right, but it goes again all my da hammered into me about looking after t'womanfolk. Don't take too long, eh?"

"We'll be in and out in a jiffy." Mrs P placed her hands on Sydney's shoulders and turned him towards the open doorway. "Now, go."

She waited until he closed the door behind himself. "Where do we start?"

"Desk? Look for a safe?" Cairstine suggested.

"The blasted desk is locked," Mrs P said as she tugged at the only drawer. "We should have kept Sydney and his lock-picking skills."

"No need." Cairstine took out another hairpin and prayed her chignon was still secure. "I didn't want to upset Sydney, but lock-picking is one of the non-womanly skills I've had since an early age. Duncan of course showed me and then, once I was faster than him, wished he hadn't." She knelt down and attacked the lock. With a grating noise, it turned. She opened the drawer.

"Empty," she said in disgust as she ran her hands around the inside, but then a thought occurred to her and she pulled the drawer completely out of the desk.

Before she could turn it over, Mrs P warned, "Shhh..."

Cairstine pushed the drawer back into place and looked around the room. There were no curtains to hide behind or even a convenient potted plant.

"What should we do?" Mrs P said. "Brazen it out?"

A voice sounded beside them. "*Psst.*"

Cairstine swung around and an unnoticed door, in what she had assumed was a fixed bookcase, swung open.

"This way." Sydney appeared and beckoned. "Be quick."

"Come on." Cairstine grabbed Mrs P's hand and dragged her over to where Sydney stood. She pushed Mrs P though the aperture and followed her, just as the door they had entered by began to open.

Sydney swung the secret door shut behind them. "There's loads of these all over the 'ouse. For us servants to get about the place."

Cairstine hardly dared breathe as heavy footsteps entered the study and she heard Armstrong's voice. Beside her, Mrs P clutched her arm tightly, and behind them Sydney's tall figure was a welcome presence.

"I could have sworn I left the book here. It was on the desk."

Cairstine couldn't remember anything on the desk except dust.

"Sir, I believe you are leading me on a wild goose chase." Duncan's voice was calm and even. "First you thought you heard someone in the hallway. Then you were sure you saw someone come into this room, which as we can both see is empty."

"Ha, but maybe not, eh?" There was the sound of a chair falling. "You think I'm stupid enough to leave it handy, eh? I'm not and I will get what I want." His voice rose. "I will, I tell you..."

Sydney put his fingers to his lips and gestured them to head down the corridor. As much as she wanted to stay and listen, Cairstine saw the wisdom of the actions. It was more than likely that Armstrong knew of the servants' corridor and at any moment might choose to open the door to it. Best to move.

They followed Sydney and he opened another door at the corridor's end. Cairstine walked by him and wondered where on earth they would find themselves now. Mrs P followed her and began to laugh. It was the sitting room they had been in earlier.

"Tea, ladies?" Sydney winked. "I'll fetch it for you dir"—the door between the sitting room and the hallway flew open so violently it bounced on its hinges—"ectly," he finished as he took a step back out of the way of the swinging door.

"Where is it?" Armstrong screeched as he bounded into the room. "You are the only persons to have been out of my sight this evening. You've taken it." He advanced on Cairstine with his fingers twitching. "I'll damn well have it back if it's the last thing I'll do. Your bloody ancestors took everything. You owe me, you..." He began to froth at the mouth. "I will..."

Cairstine stepped backwards as he advanced towards her. Duncan entered the room at a run. "Touch one hair on my wife's head, sir, and I promise you will regret it for the rest of your miserable life."

"Wife? She can't be your wife... She has to be ours..." The words were nigh on unrecognisable, but the fury in which they were spoken was unmistakeable. "She is for Geo...George..."

Cairstine glanced around the room. What would be a good weapon to defend herself? She was in no doubt she would need something.

A strident male voice shouted from the doorway, "Enough, Father. This madness ends here and now. I took the letter and handed it to Lord McColl, who saw fit to burn it, I'm glad to say."

Cairstine recognised the speaker's voice from the night they had all stayed at the Bay Horse Inn.George Armstrong. Relief flooded through her as Gordon Armstrong sank to his knees and began to rock.

"How could you? I needed it. *You* needed it. We are ruined. Ruined, I say. You have let this happen."

His son crossed the room to him. "Father, I do not want the letter or need it at all. This is your idea of retribution for an imagined slight, not mine. All our fortunes require to improve is good management. I will work harder to ensure they will. You'll see. Now come away and let Dooley help you to bed." He nodded to the footman, who helped the distraught Gordon Armstrong to his feet and along with Sydney led him from the room, still sobbing.

"My apologies, Lady McColl." George bowed. "My father has been failing for some time now. I shall seek specialist medical help for him. Indeed, I would have done so before had I realised to what lengths he would go."

Duncan put his arm around her waist and she leant against him gratefully. However, the surprises of the evening were not over. Duncan squeezed her gently. "Hold up, my love. All will soon be over."

Cairstine smiled and was about to speak when the door to the hallway opened.

Her father walked into the room.

"Papa? Is it really you?"

"It really is."

George smiled. "I arrived in Scotland to find His Grace preparing to depart in the opposite direction. Once the matter of the letter had been amicably resolved between us, we decided to travel to Corbridge in each other's company."

Cairstine ran to her father and kissed his cheek. "Papa. I'm happy that you're here."

He squeezed her hand. "As am I, and happier still that this business is done with. We can return home and resume our normal life."

Cairstine felt her cheeks heat a little. Now came the tricky part. "Well...not quite. Duncan and I...er, became handfast before we ourselves travelled south. I will be returning home to Scotland, but as his wife."

Her papa looked over her head at Duncan. "Oh, so you finally stepped up to the plate then, did you? You could have saved us all a deal of trouble had you done so earlier."

Duncan stood straighter, made no excuse nor apologised. "As could the letter for never having been written in the first place, Your Grace. As to the rest, my wife understands the why and wherefore of my proposal and there, as far as I'm concerned, the subject ends."

Nathaniel McColl's face relaxed and, knowing her father as she did, Cairstine suspected her husband had just passed a test. His son-in-law had stood his ground and stated their credentials to be recognised as a married couple. "All right, all right. Don't poker up so. All's well that ends well—other than you'll formalise your union to be legal in the rest of the kingdom with the same amount of urgency, I hope?"

Duncan nodded. "I'll ride to Newcastle and obtain a special licence from the bishop tomorrow."

Cairstine looked around for Mrs P. who, like any chaperone worth her salt, seemed to have faded into the background when not required to contribute to the proceedings. She crossed her fingers and told a small white lie to soothe her papa's ruffled feathers when she spotted her standing quietly beside George Armstrong. "And I've been chaperoned to observe the proprieties while in England, Papa. Dear Mrs P, ah…I mean, Mrs Percival-Smyth has been staying with us at Denny House."

Papa turned his head in Mrs P's direction. His face flushed and he took a firm hold on the back of a nearby chair. "Evanna…? You're here? How…?"

Mrs P, now as pale as the holland covers in the nearby rooms, curtseyed without smiling. Her face was blank and guarded. "I am, Your Grace. Although now you are too, my job is done." She beckoned to Sydney, who was back and now loitered at the door, watching with his mouth open. "Sydney, jump to it. Walk me home."

Cairstine looked firstly at her friend, then her father, trying to grasp the meaning of their reactions on seeing each other. "Mrs P…?" she asked. "Are you not returning with us to Denny House?"

Mrs P's face relaxed to smile at her. "You have no need of me now your papa has arrived, my love. Indeed, the fact that he has makes my residence at Denny House inappropriate."

"Because you're both currently unmarried as such? Papa being a widower and you a widow?" It sounded a load of hogwash to Cairstine. Her papa appeared poleaxed and Mrs P unable to look in his direction. She glanced towards Duncan, who shrugged. It seemed he had no clue as to what was going on either.

Mrs P nodded. "That is the sum of it. I will see you before you leave." She walked to the door, curtsied her farewell to the company and turned away. Cairstine couldn't be sure, but thought she heard a soft murmur as she left the room with Sydney one pace behind her. "If it were only that..."

* * * *

Duncan glanced around the room, took in the expressions on everyone's faces and stepped forwards to take charge of the situation. His wife looked confused and his father-in-law stunned as they stared at Mrs P's retreating back. *Enough is enough.* For one evening anyway. The butler hovered in the hallway, so he beckoned to him. "Summon our carriage, please. It's late and I'm sure His Grace and Mr Armstrong need some rest following their strenuous journey from the north." He offered George his hand in friendship as the butler hurried away to do his bidding. "I thank and honour you, sir. For your intervention in this matter."

George accepted with a hearty shake. "I sincerely apologise for my parent's actions and while to hope you'll forgive him is too much to expect, I would beg to offer a little understanding of how he came to be as he is?"

Cairstine drew closer to listen, so Duncan nodded and George continued.

"Laudanum was prescribed for a youthful malady which restored his well-being to such an extent that it was used to treat all subsequent ailments thereafter. It was a gradual process, his addiction. A few drops here and there, once or twice a year, then a few drops a month until after twenty years it's become many drops several times a day. Combined with a liking for strong spirits, his mind has become addled. Tall stories become the truth and an appreciation of real life diminishes."

"I've heard Lord Byron is similarly afflicted," Duncan said. "A sorry state of affairs."

George agreed. "I believe so." He bowed to Cairstine. "I apologise for your having to encounter my father when I was from home, but I had no knowledge you were the ward, Lord Callander, or should I say, Sir David Livermore, was escorting when I met him at the Bay Horse. If I'd known you were travelling to Corbridge I would not have left my father here without me."

"We had no inkling you were not a willing part of his scheme so did not make ourselves known. For all we knew you were heading north to put further pressure on my father," Cairstine replied.

The duke smiled ruefully. "If not for the seriousness of what was being attempted, I'd call it a comedy of errors. All could have been solved within a minute on an exchange of names. Still, to borrow another line from the bard, 'what's done is done'."

"Lady Macbeth, act two, scene three," Cairstine ventured.

Her father nodded.

Cairstine smiled. "I remember winter afternoons snug in the library at home in front of a roaring fire. You reading aloud from the works of Shakespeare. Assuming the character's voices to hold my interest in the archaic language."

The butler walked into the room and announced, "My lords and lady, your carriage awaits."

Duncan offered Cairstine his arm. "Then to quote another line from the play, 'What is done cannot be undone. To bed, to bed, to bed.' None of us has suffered any lasting harm. A new day and fresh start await us on the morrow."

He led Cairstine to the coach and she yawned as she settled back against the squabs. "Goodness. I find myself quite worn out after all the excitement."

Duncan thought her father looked the same. The duke sat quietly, his gaze unfocused, staring vacantly into the far corner of the coach. "Are you quite well, Your Grace?"

His father-in-law blinked. "Yes, yes. It was a shock, of course… I'll take a light supper and a restorative brandy in my room. Think on matters quietly. Set them right in my mind."

Cairstine squeezed his hand. "Yes, you should, Papa. I'll take you up as soon as we arrive at Denny House. It will have to be a room roadside, I'm afraid. Dear Mrs P's things are still in the one beside my own."

"Ah…they are?"

Cairstine nodded. "I'll call on her tomorrow to make arrangements for them to collected."

"Won't you be a little busy? I believe we have an occasion to attend." Duncan grinned.

Cairstine waved an airy hand. "You, my love, have a journey to and from Newcastle to make. I shall visit while you do so, and also invite Mrs P to attend the church. She's been so kind and supportive I declare our wedding day would not be the same without her."

Duncan smiled. "I agree."

The coach halted. As promised, Cairstine showed her father up the stairs after asking Chollerford for a bowl of soup, bread, cheese and the brandy decanter. Duncan walked into the sitting room, poured two stiff drams and waited for Cairstine to join him. She did so and sniffed the glass appreciatively when he handed it her. "Perfect. I've settled Papa in a comfortable chair. He looks quite knocked up."

Duncan nodded. "I'm not surprised. It's quite a trek from where we live in Scotland to Corbridge."

They relaxed and sipped, sat side by side on the sofa, until Cairstine's eyelids began to droop. He kissed the top of head. "Come, my love. You're done in. Up to bed with you."

She tilted her face and urged his closer, her soft pink lips slightly parted. He threaded his fingers through the length of her hair and kissed her long and deep, their first in what seemed forever. Their tongues meshed and Cairstine moaned soft and low into his mouth. His groin reacted, hardening, pushing against the material of his breeches. He broke their kiss. "Away with you, you hussy. You'll have my desire on display for all to see in a public room."

She brushed her fingertips over his throbbing crotch, stood and blew him a playful kiss. "Be in my room in half an hour, my lord. For if you're not, be assured I'll be banging on the door of your own demanding my wifely rights."

He chuckled as she left the sitting room and willed his unruly member to behave. It softened slightly, so he took his chance to dash to his bedroom and change into his rather less-revealing banyan. Robbie knocked and entered as he donned it. From the grin on his face

Duncan guessed the servants' grapevine at the Armstrong house was as good as any.

"Well, that's a turn-up for the book, my lord. Armstrong Senior is as mad as a March Hare, but thankfully his son is a man of principle."

"George is a man of honour, no doubt. I will do what I can to promote his interests going forwards, as I'm sure will Lady Callander's father. I need to ride to Newcastle in the morning, but we have only carriage horses here. Visit the ostler and rent a fast hack first thing?"

Robbie nodded. "Aye. I'll wake you when I have."

"If I'm not here, knock at my wife's room."

"Aye."

Duncan padded across the landing and let himself into Cairstine's room. A single oil lamp provided enough light to show him she was beneath the covers of the bed. She gazed at him and ran the tip of her tongue over her top lip. "Take it off."

He lifted his banyan over his head and revealed his nakedness, his cock standing stiff and proud. "And you."

She pushed the coverlet back and his mouth ran dry when he saw she had not bothered to don a night-rail. The pink nipples of her pert, round breasts were hard, the auburn curls of her muff glistened with her arousal. She parted her legs. "You want?"

*Oh, God…yes…*

Duncan moved to the bed, plunged his face between her thighs and she writhed beneath him as he sucked, and nibbled, and explored with his tongue every intimate crease on offer. She knotted her fingers through the back of hair and tugged. "I want your cock in my mouth…now."

He groaned, straddled her and offered his engorged cockhead to her lips. She grasped his length and sucked, moving her hand back and forth until he tensed, his seed threatening to burst forth. She spread her legs wider. "Take me..."

He stroked through her wet muff, replaced his fingers with his shaft and thrust. She moaned as his length filled her. "Duncan...yes...more..."

He grasped her buttocks, held her to him and pumped harder and faster until she dug her fingertips into his shoulders, then lowered his head and sucked hard on her nipple. She cried out. "Oh, yes, yes yes..." His climax exploded.

They stilled, breathing hard, and he held her to his chest when he rolled away. Cairstine sighed and drowsed in his arms. "We can be in bed together every night now...and perhaps some afternoons."

He smiled and patted her buttocks. "Insatiable minx."

She snuggled closer. "Yes... Wake me in the morning and I'll ring for Tansy to bring us a dish of coffee or hot chocolate each."

Their rest did not last long enough for either of them to fall asleep. An urgent tattoo beat on the door, just as they began to snuggle together again, sent Duncan bolt upright. Cairstine brushed her hair out of her eyes, fumbled across the covers and pulled on her night-rail.

"My lord! My lord! The Armstrongs' house is ablaze!"

Duncan tugged on his banyan and rushed to open the door. Robbie stood on the other side of it, urgency writ clear on his face. "Flames have burst all the windows, my lord. The roof won't withstand them for long."

"Has a bucket chain been formed from the river?" Duncan barked as he reached for his breeches and shirt. "Are all the occupants out?"

"Dunno as to people, but the chain is there. It ain't dousing it though..."

Duncan shoved his feet into his boots and headed for the hallway. "My love, I need to find buckets."

"Just go! I'll meet you downstairs as soon as I'm decent," Cairstine called from behind him. There was no time to dally.

She was as good as her word and beat him to the front door, a pelisse thrown over a plain front-buttoned day dress. Her papa, still dressed in his day clothes, was with her.

Duncan thrust some blankets into her arms and gave several buckets to her papa.

"Wet the blankets to smother flames," he said as they all ran outside and followed Robbie at a trot. "No idea what else we'll need till we get there."

The imminent inferno was not long coming into view and it was a welcome sight to see George and his father stood streetside outside the conflagration, surrounded by their staff.

As one they halted and stared at the devastation, then moved closer to comfort George. His father did not react well to the sight of them. He tore his wig from his head, jumped up and down on it and laughed wildly. "Think to ruin me, do you, eh? Well, you shan't. There's nothing left. I've made sure of it..." He struggled and broke free of George's hold then ran into the flames with a screech. "The McColl curse is finally broken!"

Duncan pulled Cairstine to him and shielded her from the sight of a man running to his doom. George moved to follow his father and Robbie held him back. "Och. It's of no use, sir."

Behind him Duncan heard a wild sob and a distraught figure dashed past him. "Nathan, I feared you were still inside..."

His father-in-law opened his arms and Mrs P, a cloak thrown over her nightgown, her hair loose down her back, moved into them. He held her close.

"There, there, my sweet. No harm done. I'm here."

"I feared I had lost you again."

Cairstine lifted her head. "Papa...?"

The duke patted Mrs P's back. "You'll excuse me, child, if I leave you in your husband's care. I must escort Evanna home."

Cairstine stared after them, a small smile upon her lips. "Why didn't I guess? I think I knew it..."

Duncan looked at Robbie. "Give George your support to Denny House, please?"

Robbie draped his arm around George's shoulders, urged him into a walk and asked, "Are we still riding to Newcastle in the morning, my lord?"

Duncan looked at George, who nodded. "He's at peace now. It is ended."

He smiled. "Why, yes we are. The vicar of St. Andrew's doesn't know it yet, but he will be conducting a wedding tomorrow..."

## Want to see more from these authors? Here's a taster for you to enjoy!

# The Scots and the Sassenachs: The Baron's Saving Grace

## Raven McAllan & Cassie O'Brien

### *Excerpt*

The inn was well presented, had a good menu and served excellent ale. To say nothing of a supply of whisky that he was certain had never been within the scent of an excise man.

George Armstrong, who, following the death of his father now bore the title Baron Hexham, winced at the squawk the feet of his chair made as he pushed it back a few inches to allow him to cross one knee over the other and not upturn the nearby table. He sniffed the spirit in his glass, savoured the peaty aroma with appreciation and took a sip.

"Douglas 'tis as good as ever," he said to the anxiously awaiting landlord. "You are a genius in securing something so special. What I wouldn't do for a cask of this at home." He laughed at the landlord's agonised expression. "No, I will not ask you to facilitate that. I imagine it is fraught enough getting sufficient for you needs."

"That it is, indeed, my lord. But if you wish, I…"

George took pity on the man. He had been only half serious when he'd said he wished he had some at home.

It would put the noses out of joint of the people who worked on his estate and had their own stills secreted away. They may lie south of the border, but their appreciation, and copying of the water of life, was alive and kicking. He had no idea where they hid the still whose results he regularly acquired, but he hoped it was never discovered by the powers that be. The resultant whisky from it was as good as the one he now savoured. "Do not worry yourself. It's another good reason to visit you. Along with your wife's cooking and a comfortable bed on my journey."

"That's grand. May I ask how t'house is comin' on?"

George sighed. His Corbridge home had been razed to the ground by his laudanum-addicted father, and in the ensuing fire his addlepated sire had perished. "Slowly, Douglas, very slowly. The one redemption from the whole sorry state is no one but the late baron was hurt, and that only when he ventured too close to the flames." He chose not to mention the man had been as naked as a jay and waving a bottle of port, *or* that he could never forgive himself for not remembering that whilst under the influence, Gordon, his late father, was irrational and likely to fall into a rage. The conflagration had been because George had foiled his parent's plans to ruin a man who, in his father's words, stole the woman Gordon had wanted. Not loved—just *wanted*—many years before. That was the manner of man he was. George hoped and prayed he had none of the man's unpleasant traits in him. "He thought he saw someone or something inside." A lie, but who was to confront him over it?

"Ah, good man, sorry ending." The landlord shook his head in sorrow. "Life must go on though, eh? You off north?" Douglas' voice penetrated George's mind and he brought himself back to the present.

George nodded. "To the Trossachs to see a good friend who lives there. Then I'm away to the Tay for the fishing before the season ends."

"Then I'll wish ye well," Douglas replied. "Not that I'd be wantin' to go so far m'sen but I know you gentry folk are happy wi all t'travel. Will you be using the private parlour later this evening?"

Amused at the idea that only those higher up the social ladder travelled, George blinked at the change of topic and considered the question while also pondering the types of people who also travelled. What about salesmen? Servants changing jobs? Drovers, herders and itinerants? The list could be endless. He mentally laughed at himself and let the thoughts go.

As to his present abode, he was comfortable where he was. The room was aptly named the snug. Three tables, two benches and four highbacked armchairs with padded seats. Set in front of a crackling fire and a bell pull for service. What more could he want? Except for a warm and willing body. That was as unlikely as a Stuart returning to the throne. "Not if you need it for someone else. I'll be as happy here."

"Then I'll tell the gentleman who wishes to use it with his ward that he may." The landlord sounded relived. "The lass has had a touch of nausea after travelling, so they're biding the night. Last two rooms, they got. We're mighty busy this day. The sheep sales, you know."

George nodded. Not that he did know a lot, but he'd intended to take a look at the sales and see if there was anything that interested him. His estate in the Cheviots would stand a few additions to the flock, and Callum his shepherd was due the following day to look the animals over. They'd been told some of a flock with an outstanding pedigree would be up for auction. A couple of rams and an ewe or two wouldn't go amiss.

George would leave everything to Callum, hand him the cash they had decided on, and keep well away. Callum was an unknown in the area – George himself was not. He wouldn't put it past some farmers to collaborate to push the prices up if it was known he was bidding. His father hadn't shown their family in a good light in the area. George accepted he would have an uphill struggle to rectify it.

He settled down in front of the fire, legs crossed at the ankle, and steepled his hands on his chin. Deep in thought, he studied the flames for a while and pondered on how fire could be both good – there at that moment – and bad – the way his home had ended up as ashes. With another dram and several of the landlady's delicious singing hinnies he contemplated all he needed to do in the next few weeks. Singing hinnies – sweet griddle cakes, which George, along with a large percentage of the local population, was partial to – were a local favourite and every cook guarded their own specific recipe jealously.

As he studied the flames, George's mind moved from the future to the past as he mused over the previous twelve months. They had been frenetic, worrying and thankfully at times, uplifting. With the exception of the fire and the tragedy of his father's death, there had been more positives than negatives, and at last George felt his life was on an even keel.

Apart of course from still being unwed. Not something that had overly bothered him in the past, but now seeing new – but good – friends happily settled, he was aware he too would like a wife. Children. A family. An heir.

How he was to achieve that he had no idea. His estate was remote and he had no interest in scouring the marriage mart anywhere. Add to that, his father's antics plus his own once well-deserved but no longer relevant reputation as a rake would go against any well-bought-up lady—or her parents—considering him as a good bet for a husband.

He sighed and stared into his tankard of ale as if it had all the answers.

It didn't. He took one mouthful, twisted the tankard around and watched the contents froth. How long before it fell flat? A bit like he felt at that moment.

George was not the sort of person to think every solution was found in the bottom of a jug of ale or a flagon of whisky and had no idea how long it was before he became aware of voices from the adjoining room. Seconds probably. He put his drink down and debated whether to scrape his chair over the floor to show the occupants that the parlour, despite its name, wasn't all that private.

Whether it was due to the way the chimneys met and merged or because the door was ill-fitted he had no idea, but two voices could be clearly heard.

"I told you I'll come with you and marry you, so why all this farridaddle?" a female voice asked. "If you don't think I'll be true to my word, lock me in my room. Try to make me share yours and I'll bring the roof down and cause such a scandal you won't have a hope of your plot succeeding. Your choice."

"You better be on the level."

George decided not to announce his presence and narrowed his eyes as if by doing so he could see though walls or even identify the speaker. Did he know him? He certainly had never heard the female voice before, but the deeper baritone sounded familiar.

"I am as on the level as you are," the lady—he was certain she *was* a lady, a gently reared female—continued. "I would do nothing to harm my family, even if you are not so scrupulous. I will not let any scandal stick to Papa or the memory of my late mama, and you know that fine well. Otherwise, you wouldn't have thought up this insidious plan. One, I might add, only a scoundrel would choose to carry out. Now, kindly go and locate the landlord and discover which room I have been allocated so I may retire for the evening. *Alone.*"

For a few seconds there was silence then the male answered.

"Very well. Wait here. But remember..." The tone George supposed was meant to be menacing had more than a hint of a whine in it. And *now* he recognised it.

*Adrian Corbett, by God. That blackguard. What is he up to?*

"Oh I remember it all. You can be sure I will go to my room, but do not think to accompany me to it, because if you do, I will..." There was a pregnant pause. "Create. A. Scene."

George mentally applauded the lady. Not many well-bred females of his admittedly limited acquaintance would have the sense—or temerity—to do so.

A door creaked open and footsteps sounded on the wooden boards of the hallway outside the snug. George considered not just the words he'd overheard but also the disdain and loathing in the female's voice. Whoever the lady may be, she was obviously being coerced into a marriage against her natural inclination. She had sounded feistily determined to stand her ground, but would her words be enough to hold at man like Adrian Corbett at bay should he decide to enter her room after imbibing a couple of brandies?

The thought turned George's stomach. The man was certainly foul enough to physically force his presence on a slighter-built female. Would probably excuse himself doing so without a second thought if she was destined to be his wife. It was not to be born. No female should be forced into marriage. With anyone. He set his glass on the table, walked quickly to the door and left the room.

* * * *

Grace Foston stared at the back of the parlour door as it closed behind the detestable Adrian Corbett and discovered she was breathing heavily, almost as if she had been out for a long hard gallop on her favourite pony then swum in the river. Both things which were frowned upon in the circles she moved in.

*The bloody man.* The gall and, she allowed, the cleverness, he showed. Her poor, poor, sister.

In Corbett's absence she re-tied and tightened the ribbons of the poke bonnet she had selected that morning for the fact of it having a large-rounded brim that shaded the top half of her face. And just in time. For not two minutes after her nemesis departed the door handle turned again. The landlord must have been hovering nearby. However, to her surprise it was not Corbett who entered the parlour but a man she had never seen before in her life. He beckoned her towards him then held out his hand.

"Come. Quick. Before he returns."

This not being part of Grace's masterplan in the slightest, she stood but moved no closer. "Ah…this is a private parlour, Sir. I request you leave it."

The man's tone became more urgent as he walked towards her. "No. No. I won't have it. Especially not with him."

Grace glared and opened her mouth to object, but before she could speak, found herself captured in a bear hug and lifted from her feet.

"Forgive me, but I cannot allow you to stay here with such a man."

Held in an embrace so tight there was no room to so much as wriggle, Grace couldn't find enough breath to scream.

What could she do?

The handle of the furled parasol she'd hung on the back of her chair brushed against her hand as he began to walk towards the door. She curled her fingers around its handle and managed to take it with her as she was carried unceremoniously from the parlour and up the stairs.

Each firm footstep echoed in her mind. Like the steps to doom.

*Stop being fanciful,* she chided herself. *Doom is not allowed in this establishment, or in my foreseeable future.* She hoped.

The man set her back on her feet and released her after toeing a bedroom door shut behind them. Grace seized her chance and set about him with her silk-covered sunshade. He yelped at the first blow. The whalebone shaft shattered at the second, and the delicate ivory sticks of its ribs disintegrated as she pummelled his arms. He held his hands up to protect his head from further assault.

"Damnation, woman. Stop it, you hellcat. I'm saving you from a fate worse than death, here. Ow! That hurt. Why did I even bother...?"

His words gave Grace pause. She surveyed the mangled parasol and dropped it with a thud. It would never be the same. "Now look what you've made me do. It's ruined. Who are you and what on earth made you step forwards as you did?" She glanced around for something near at hand that could also be used as a weapon. Two vases and a heavy, ugly statue of a naked nymph could be easily reached. Reassured, she stared at the man. "I demand an explanation at once." She stamped her foot. "And I mean it, or else." What a stupid statement. Or else *what*? "Explanation. Now."

She was not at all certain she'd get one. Handsome, engaging, and no doubt a rake, he wouldn't be the sort of person to tamely reply. He had the look about him. A man to do as he preferred and not kowtow to conformity.

The intruder rubbed his head where she could see a lump was already forming. He smiled, ruefully. "George Armstrong. At your service and to rescue you from the clutches of a man no sane person would spend a minute with. Otherwise, it won't only be the parasol that is ruined." He held out his hand. "If you wish to escape him, come with me now. We don't have a lot of time."

She ignored it and resolutely tamped down the hint of sympathy for the injury she had bestowed on him. He deserved it. His face might be unfamiliar, but his name was not. The antics of a certain Mr G A of Corbridge had made regular appearances in the scandal sheets over the years. Why on earth hadn't she kept her pistol in her reticule instead of stowing it in her portmanteau? She glanced towards the most substantial vase in the room. She would have no chance to reach it before he overpowered her. The nymph it would have to be. She had an irrelevant thought of the statue's prominent breasts hitting him in a place he would find *very* painful.

"George Armstrong... I've heard of you."

He winced as if the note of disgust in her voice pained him. Why? His reputation as a first-class rebrobate was a matter of public record after all. .

"I should have hit your harder," Grace said forcefully. "As it is my poor parasol will never be opened again. Who are you to tell how me to go on? You... you... rake..." She didn't add that she had also heard of his prowess as a lover, although being face to face with his broad shoulders and undoubted good looks she had no trouble believing the truthfulness of those particular rumours. Not that she intended to let it influence her. Not at all. So why was every nerve end tingling, her palms clammy and her brain sending amorous thought to her brain? Along the lines of 'wouldn't it be good to find out'?

*Enough. Concentrate on the necessities of this situation.*

His mouth quirked up at the corners and a twinkle entered his blue eyes as if what she had just said amused him.

"A rake?" he drawled, in the best rakish voice she had heard in an age. "I'm not sure I'd go so far as to call myself that, not these days at any rate, although I will admit to the odd peccadillo or several in my past. Due to those ah...interesting times, and given my youthful follies, I have experience of how a rake's mind works. I've met many a man like Corbett. I hope not to meet many more, but I don't hold my breath. They seem to go forth and multiply at a formidable rate."

Grace looked longingly at the nymph once again then glared at him. *Youthful follies? Not if the papers were to be believed. Is he addled?*

"Are you an aficionado of the poppy, Mr Armstrong?" It was the most scathing thing she could think of on the spur of the moment.

Any hint of humour fled from George's face. He reddened.

*Maybe that was a bit too much. He appears ready to commit murder. Probably mine.* Grace opened her mouth to apologise, but before she had a chance to speak, he beat her to it.

"I am not," he replied stiffly. "I have no need of such things, be they medicinal or not. As for Corbett, I have no clue as to whether he has any unsavoury addiction, although what I do know about him is that he's a less than honourable man. A weasel. A reprobate of the first order. An underhand rogue." He raised his shoulders and let them fall. "Count your fingers after he has held your hand. The type of person whose only consideration is for himself and what is best for him. Nothing else. Why on earth is someone like you here with someone like him?" His voice was desolate and his bleak expression made her wince.

However, she was wise enough to know any sympathy would not, at that given moment, be well received. Grace held her tongue, striving not to let her temper get the better of her and fairly sure she would not succeed. After all, what did he know?

Given his father's sad history the lady's question had stung, although she would not realise why it had caused him pain. Her next words had him within an inch of showing her the door and leaving her to fend for herself, but he could not bring himself to do it. No female should be left in Corbett's clutches, let alone one quite as tempting as the apple-cheeked beauty stood in front of him now.

"This is folly," he said in what he hoped was a reasonable tone and suspected she would disagree. "Someone needs to tell you."

She pursed the perfect bow of her lips. "So, you say."

*She disagreed. God save me from a bloody contrary woman. Even if she does make my body tighten and my cock stretch my breeches.*

"As I've told you. I *know* so."

*And if you believe different you deserve all you get.*

"Your opinion, Sir, is nothing I need to have regard for." She clenched her fists. George watched her warily. Women could be unpredictable, he knew that to his cost from his past. This one, he already knew, had a strong arm and could use it to great success. It would be preferable if she didn't have cause to use it in his direction in the future.

"I am damned sure you do, woman. I rescued you."

The lady sent a glowering glance in his direction. One silk-slipper shod foot beat a soft but determined staccato rhythm on the carpeted floor.

"Do not call me *woman* in that tone, *Sir*."

How had she made 'Sir' sound a like an epithet?

"I didn't need rescuing," the lady went on in the same 'explaining to a simpleton' tone. "My sister and I are similar enough in looks for me to fool Corbett into thinking I am her. Especially when aided by a large-brimmed bonnet and parasol to hide the fact that my eyes are green rather than blue and my hair is lighter in colour than hers."

George couldn't help himself and grinned. It sounded interesting and took his mind away from his problems. "Why on earth would you need to do that?"

She eyed him in a considering way, as if making up her mind about him. Did she think him untrustworthy?

"For my ears only," he added. "I might appear someone who shares but trust me I do not." He chuckled. "No rake or rogue worth their salt would gossip, and no ex-rake doubly so."

Then she nodded, plonked herself down on the padded boudoir chair with a sigh and removed her head gear. She tossed it onto the floor and pressed her fingers to her temples as if to massage away pain. Should he ask if she had the headache? Perhaps not. She night say yes and he was the one who caused it.

"Ahh, that's better. Let me try and explain. Around seven years ago, Mama passed away in tragic circumstances—she slipped and fell into a river swollen with winter rains, caught pneumonia and died within days. Not long after Papa re-married. He's one of those men who need to have a wife. I've never been quite sure why. After all, half the time he's not at home. Which is by the by. My sister, Jane, still resides at the family home and our stepmother resents this. She wants her gone. It interferes with her social life." Her lips curled. "Including the, ah…how should I put it…"

"Shenanigans? Peccadillos?" George nodded. "It happens."

"Sadly. As you say. My poor papa. To make matters worse, you will find Corbett's name on my stepmother's family tree, albeit on a different branch. Jane and I believe if she's not actually in cahoots with Corbett, she has encouraged and aided his pretentions to Jane's hand."

George pulled the high-backed chair from the desk and sat on it. "Why? Is Jane a great heiress or something?"

The lady's smile, although rueful, lit her face and nearly took George's breath away. "No. We each have a small dowry along with a few hundred pounds inherited from Mama to be given to us on the day we marry. Corbett's obsession with Jane is purely lust, I fear."

If the sister was in anyway comparable with the lady sat opposite him, George could see why Corbett desired her. Another's encouragement coupled with the man's own shady morals clarified for him how the situation had come to be. Apart from one point. "Ah…so two sisters alike in looks and circumstances. What makes you an unacceptable alternative to Jane?"

"Alike in looks? Enough, unless we are stood side-by-side, but Corbett has never seen me in person so it does not naturally occur to him that Jane is not Jane. A few theatricals on my part have kept him on his toes and his mind rather too busy to think it through. Alike in circumstances? Not at all. Jane is unwed because she has been waiting for the man she loves to return from active duty. When she got wind of what Corbett was plotting, she appealed to the colonel of his regiment, who luckily was a distant relative to our mama. The upshot being Major Winterbottom has been granted a period of compassionate leave. If my delaying tactics work according to plan, they will arrive at Gretna ahead of myself and Corbett. When we ourselves get there, Corbett will discover Jane is now married, and he is in the company of the wrong sis…"

Her words trailed off at the sound of a tap on the door. It opened and the landlord walked into the room, his arms full of logs for the fire. Douglas' eyes widened as surveyed George's female companion and his face reddened. "Um. Please accept apologies, my lord. I didn't realise you had, ah…company."

He deposited the logs in a wicker basket beside the grate, lit the oil lamps on the mantle with a taper flamed in the fire and backed hastily out of the room.

*That's done it! There's only one honourable way out of this.*

George opened his mouth to speak the words and found they came easily, as if this was his destiny. The way it was always meant to be. "Would you do me the great honour of becoming my wife?" He waited for her answer with bated breath.

Her face softened. "How very kind of you, but I'm afraid my answer must be no. Perhaps by way of an explanation I could offer you my name?"

George's heart sank. He nodded as his mouth went dry. He suspected he was in for an unpleasant surprise.

"The Honourable Mrs Roger Foston."

He was correct.

*Mrs? Roger Foston? But he's even older than my father would be now...*

Whatever else he had expected to hear it was not this. Eloquence fled. Instead of a polite 'pleased to meet you' only two words escaped his mouth. "How? Why?"

He received an amused smile accompanied by a shrug. "How? Well, in the normal manner. Roger proposed and I accepted. We were wed in the local church a few weeks later. Why? Well, there are worse situations to find oneself in than to be wed to a good-natured man who treats his wife with respect, and understands not all women are without a brain, and that some need more from life than an endless round of parties and tittle-tattle."

In the face of her refreshingly candid reply, George gathered his scattered wits and walked to a long side table. He had investigated the contents of the decanters earlier before descending the stairs to spend the evening in the snug. He poured a glass of ratafia for her, and a large tot of whisky for himself. "More than residing in a home where you are neither welcome nor wanted, for instance?"

"Amongst other things." She took the wine from him, had a sip and made a face before she put the glass down on a nearby table. "Good grief, it is revoltingly sweet. What are *you* drinking?"

He handed her his glass with a bow, fully expecting her to decline. She didn't. Instead, she lifted it to her nose, sniffed the contents and smiled in appreciation before she tasted.

"Ah, Glen Eyevie, I suspect. Good choice. I do wonder how on earth it arrived here? Old Angus McSporran is very careful whom he selects to be a recipient of his talents, and his very words I believe are 'he cannae stand most o' thon sassenachs'." She laughed. "You appear surprised I know such things? My husband is happy to introduce me to such niceties as a good malt. We may be sassenachs, but we both have ancestors from north of the border."

He nodded but made no comment regarding her or her husband's antecedents, instead content to keep things harmonious and to the point.

"A fine whisky for a fine lady." He poured himself a fresh measure. "*Slàinte*. Your husband is obviously a man of discerning taste, Mrs Foston." He hoped she didn't understand the underlying implications in his words, or if she did accept his admiration without reservation.

She put the glass down and held out her hand. "Being as I'm in your bedroom, albeit unwillingly, you'd best call me Grace."

George shook it gently and managed the words he hadn't been capable of earlier. "Pleased to meet you, Grace, and please accept my apologies. My actions were rash but carried out with the best of intentions in mind."

A challenging glint entered her eyes. "Rash? Certainly. For the best? I have yet to make up my mind. Do you make a habit of forcibly removing females according to your own summation of their situation?"

George picked up the gauntlet and ran with it. "About as often you adopt a false persona purposefully to deceive, I suspect."

His remark hit home. Grace's face flushed.

# About the Authors

## Raven McAllan

After 30 plus years in Scotland, Raven now lives near the east Yorkshire coast, with her long-suffering husband, who is used to rescuing the dinner, when she gets immersed in her writing, keeping her coffee pot warm and making sure the wine is chilled.

With a new home to decorate and a garden to plan, she's never short of things to do, but writing is always at the top of her list.

Her other hobbies include walking along the coast and spotting the wildlife, reading, researching, cros stitch and trying not to drop stitches as she endeavours to knit.

Being left-handed, and knitting right-handed, that's not always easy.

## Cassie O'Brien

I love:

Being with family and friends.

Writing and having the freedom to do so now child four of four has passed her driving test and is off to uni later this year.

I Like:

Any excuse to throw a party.

Any excuse to open a bottle of fizz.

Shoes in vast quantities - the higher the heel the better.

Ambitions:

To write many more books.

To own a pair of Louboutin's.

To never go near an iron or a hoover again.

Raven and Cassie love to hear from readers. You can find their contact information, website details and author profile page at https://www.totallybound.com

TOTALLY
BOUND
Home of Erotic Romance

www.ingramcontent.com/pod-product-compliance
Lightning Source LLC
LaVergne TN
LVHW090945080826
845145LV00003B/901

* 9 7 8 1 8 3 9 4 3 7 4 9 6 *